A man tha
anywhere.

He'd escaped her clutches without telling her anything at all. Darn. Either he was good at deflecting or he was just as curious as she was by nature.

She couldn't make up her mind.

Then the crowd parted a bit and she could see his butt, a very nice, flat butt, cased in denim. As a female, she couldn't help but respond to the sight. Eye candy indeed.

No, Liza couldn't forget Max McKenny. Even as she nodded, listened and talked, he was the image burned in the forefront of her brain.

There was something there. And she wanted to know what it was.

But when she looked around again, he had vanished from the room.

A deflector who was good at disappearing acts? She could feel her instincts rev into high gear. Before she was finished, she was going to know everything about Max McKenny.

Dear Reader,

Having a lot of journalists in my family has given me some familiarity with their inquisitive natures and often frank questions. They're fun to listen to and they have wonderful stories to tell, but they're not quite like the rest of us. They sometimes deal with some pretty ugly things, and being suspicious seems to become second-nature.

You want to get a journalist's attention? Give them the feeling you're hiding something. Ordinarily it won't matter unless you're someone in a position of power or influence, but they can be a little tough with their curiosity and questioning even with family and friends. It seems to be built in, and then it's finely honed. They want to know everything about everything.

And that's how this story was born. I wanted a heroine with just that tart, sharp nature, that curiosity, even that hint of black humor. And then I wanted it to drag her into a dangerous situation. Being a journalist can do that, sometimes when you least expect it.

Wanting to know too much gets Liza Enders into trouble. It also gets her into love.

Enjoy!

Rachel

RACHEL LEE

Guardian in Disguise

ROMANTIC
SUSPENSE

Recycling programs
for this product may
not exist in your area.

ISBN-13: 978-0-373-27771-1

GUARDIAN IN DISGUISE

www.Harlequin.com

Printed in U.S.A.

Books by Rachel Lee

Harlequin Romantic Suspense

**The Final Mission* #1655
**Just a Cowboy* #1663
**The Rescue Pilot* #1671
**Guardian in Disguise* #1701

Silhouette Romantic Suspense

An Officer and a Gentleman #370
Serious Risks #394
Defying Gravity #430
Exile's End #449
Cherokee Thunder #463
Miss Emmaline and the Archangel #482
Ironheart #494
Lost Warriors #535
Point of No Return #566
A Question of Justice #613
Nighthawk #781
Cowboy Comes Home #865
Involuntary Daddy #955
Holiday Heroes #1487
  "A Soldier for All Seasons"
**A Soldier's Homecoming* #1519
**Protector of One* #1555
**The Unexpected Hero* #1567
**The Man from Nowhere* #1595
**Her Hero in Hiding* #1611
**A Soldier's Redemption* #1635
**No Ordinary Hero* #1643

Harlequin Nocturne

***Claim the Night* #127
***Claimed by a Vampire* #129
***Forever Claimed* #131

*Conard County
**Conard County:
    The Next Generation
***The Claiming

Other titles by this author available
in ebook format.

RACHEL LEE

was hooked on writing by the age of twelve, and practiced her
craft as she moved from place to place all over the United States.
This *New York Times* bestselling author now resides in Florida and
has the joy of writing full-time.

To inquisitive journalists everywhere,
especially some who belong to my family.
Thanks for digging for the truth.

Chapter 1

Liza Enders looked around the room at all the people gathered for the faculty welcoming tea. Yes, they called it a tea, which struck her as a grandiose description for a gathering of faculty members at a junior college in Conard County, Wyoming.

A "tea" should have paneled walls, leather chairs, old Victorian tables and heavy curtains.

Instead the faculty occupied a cafeteria with folding tables, plastic chairs and vertical blinds on the windows. The sandwiches were quartered but still had crusts, the beverage was a punch made of a soft drink poured over a brick of ice cream, and there was hot, tinny coffee in huge urns. The coffee cups were institutional, white with a green line, and the punch cups were plastic.

It was hard not to laugh.

"Tea" indeed.

She knew most of the faculty already because Conard County was her hometown and she'd already taught her first course over the summer session. This tea was the only one held each year, however, and the college didn't spring for more intimate evening gatherings with the dean. No, they held this one social each year and all faculty were required to attend.

That meant the one new guy stuck out. Of course, he would have stuck out anyway, given that he didn't remotely resemble his peers.

Most of the faculty looked like underpaid teachers, which they were. All teachers were underpaid, just as journalists were. Liza knew all about that, having recently been laid off from her job as a reporter.

They dressed casually but nobody had this dude's kind of cool. And *cool* was the only word she could think of to describe it. He stood there holding a mug of coffee without using the handle, his denim-clad hips canted to one side in a way that was going to drive his female students nuts. His black T-shirt showed off some pretty good musculature—not at all common among the bookish types —and instead of the usual faculty jogging shoes or cowboy boots, he wore black motorcycle boots. Cool, she thought again.

Her instincts, honed by a decade as a reporter, drew her in his direction. Those little differences in appearance and stance suggested an interesting story, not a curriculum vitae of academic accomplishments.

She ran her eyes over him as she eased toward him, appreciating the picture of maleness, and allowing herself to enjoy the moment of attraction. God knew, she wasn't attracted to any of the other male professors—most of whom were married, happily or not.

But she was curious. She'd spent a lot of time getting

people to tell her things, and she was sure she'd get this guy's story before this sham of a tea was over. Then her curiosity would be satisfied and she'd be able to return her attention to more serious matters. Like teaching, and figuring out what she really wanted to do with her mess of a life now that her true love, journalism, had spurned her in massive cost-saving layoffs.

That still rankled. The hunk in the black T-shirt would provide a little distraction and satisfy her now under-satisfied need to know everything about people. Especially intriguing people.

Something about this guy caused her nose for news to twitch like mad.

When she reached him, she extended her hand and gave him her friendliest smile. "Hi. I'm Liza Enders. I teach journalism."

He shook her hand, a firm grip. "Max McKenny, criminology."

That totally snagged her attention. "Really. I did the cop beat until I was promoted."

"That's a promotion? Getting away from cops?"

He smiled at last, and she was almost embarrassed by the way her heart skipped a beat. Such a good-looking man already had enough going for him without adding a devastating smile. Slightly shaggy dark hair with just a bit of wave to it, eyes the color of blue polar ice. Yummy. What was it he had just said? Oh, yeah…

"It's considered one," she finally answered. "The cop beat is rough but not all that difficult in terms of gathering information, so it's usually given to the newest reporters. Most of us don't last long at it, though."

"Why not?"

"Between the hours and the stories? Well, you teach criminology, but I also covered auto accidents."

"Oh." His smile faded a bit. "That would be rough."

"The average survival as a cop reporter is about two years," she agreed. Then it struck her: he was learning about her.

She cocked her head a little. Had she just been deflected? She didn't know many people who could do that, including crooked politicians with a lot to hide. "What about you? Law enforcement background?"

"Some," he said with a shrug. "No big deal."

"Well, your course will be popular. Seems like CSI made you a ready audience."

At that his smile returned to full wattage. "Not much reality there."

"No," she agreed. "Criminalists don't last too long on the job, either. Five years, is what some of them told me. So you were a criminalist?"

He shook his head. "Just law enforcement. I'm teaching mostly procedures and the law."

"Were you a beat cop?"

"I was on the streets, yes."

It seemed like a straightforward answer but Liza's instincts twitched again. "I always thought it would be rough to be a beat cop," she said by way of beginning a deeper probe. But just as she was framing her question he asked her one.

"So what do you get promoted to after the cop beat?"

She blinked. "Depends." Then she decided to open up a bit, hoping to get him to do the same. "I went to county government next."

"That must have been boring as hell."

"Far from it. Folks don't realize just how much impact local government has on their lives. Most of the decisions that affect an individual are made locally. Plus, it can be fun to watch."

"I can't imagine it."

"Only because you haven't done it. You see some real antics. But what about being on the beat? You must have had some nerve-racking experiences."

He shrugged one shoulder. "I had my share, I suppose. You know what they say, hours of sheer boredom punctuated by seconds of sheer terror."

"I can imagine. I bet you have some stories to tell," she suggested invitingly.

"Not really." He smiled again. "I was a lucky cop. You probably saw more bad stuff than I did."

"Well, most cops tell me they go their entire careers without ever having to draw a gun."

"That's actually true, thank God."

"So what made you change careers?"

He paused, studying her. "Reporters," he said finally, and chuckled quietly. "I'm taking a hiatus. Sometimes you need to step back for a while. You?"

God, he was almost good enough at eliciting information to be a reporter himself. No way she could ignore his question without being rude, and if she was rude she'd never learn his story.

"Laid off," she said baldly. "Didn't you hear? News is just an expense. Advertising is where the money is at."

"But…" He hesitated. "I don't know a lot about your business, but if papers don't have news, who is going to buy them? And if no one buys them…"

"Exactly. You got that exactly right. But the bean counters and the shareholders don't seem to get that part. Plus, they just keep cutting staff until every reporter is doing the work of three or four. No one cares that the quality goes down, and there's no real in-depth coverage."

"Blame it on a shortening national attention span."

"Cable news," she said.

"Thirty-second sound bites."

Suddenly they both laughed, and she decided he was likable, even if he was full of secrets. Secrets that she was going to get to the bottom of.

Although, she reminded herself, she couldn't really be sure he had secrets. It was just a feeling, and while her news sense didn't often mislead her, she might be rusty after six months. Maybe. She cast about quickly for a way to bring the conversation back to him. "Where did you work before and how did you get to this backwater?"

"I was in Michigan," he said easily. "Is this a backwater? I hadn't noticed."

She almost flushed. Was he chiding her for putting down her hometown? For an instant she thought he might not be at all likable, but before she could decide he asked her another question.

"How about you?" He tilted his head inquisitively. "What brought you here?"

"Two things. A job and the fact that I grew up here. I like this place."

"And before? Where did you work?"

"For a major daily in Florida." Damn, she was supposed to be the one asking.

"That's a big change in climate," he remarked. "I doubt I'll notice this winter as much as you will."

Before she could turn the conversation back to him, he looked away. "I'm being summoned. Nice meeting you, Ms. Enders."

"Liza," she said automatically as he started to move away.

"Max," he said over his shoulder and disappeared into the crowd.

Well, he didn't exactly disappear. A man like him couldn't disappear anywhere. Soon she saw him conversing with some other teachers.

He'd escaped her clutches without telling her anything at all. Darn. Either he was good at deflecting or he was just as curious as she was by nature.

She couldn't make up her mind.

When the crowd parted a bit, she could see his butt, a very nice butt, cased in denim. As a female, she couldn't help but respond to the sight. Eye candy indeed.

One of the other faculty members started yammering in her ear about the renewed effort to build a resort on Thunder Mountain and she reluctantly tore her gaze away.

Max wasn't handsome, she told herself as she listened politely to the man talk about the threat a resort would raise to the mountain's wolf pack.

She cared about wolves, she really did, and didn't want to see them driven away or killed.

But she couldn't forget Max McKenny. Even as she talked about wolves, he was the image burned in the forefront of her brain.

There was something there, a story of some kind. And she wanted to know what it was.

But when she looked around again, he had vanished from the room.

A deflector who was good at disappearing? Her instincts revved into high gear. Before she was done, she was going to know everything about Max McKenny.

She might have laughed at herself, but she knew exactly why she was reacting this way: training and instinct. It had been over six months since she'd had a story to follow. Max might be the most normal ex-cop on the planet, but that wasn't the point. The hunt for information was. She could hardly wait to get to her home computer.

"So will you help us?" Dexter Croft asked her. "With the petition drive?"

"I'll see what I can do," she agreed almost automatically. "But the ranchers aren't happy about those wolves, which means many of the other locals aren't, either."

"Those wolves don't get anywhere near the herds," he said irritably. "In fifteen years we've only had one confirmed wolf kill."

"I know, Dex," she said soothingly. "I know. But it's the idea we're fighting. That and the news from Montana and Idaho."

"Which is not all that bad."

"I guess that depends."

Dex drew himself up. "On what?"

"Whether you're a rancher who's running on a margin so slim one kill could cost you nearly everything."

"They get reimbursed for wolf kills."

She smothered a sigh. She wanted to save the wolves, yes, but you had to consider the other side of the story. Without cooperation from the ranchers one way or another, the wolves weren't going to make it. "I said I'd help, Dex. But maybe we need a better way to talk to the ranchers."

"We've been talking to them for years."

"Maybe the problem is we've been talking at them. I don't know. But I said I'd help."

She turned to scan the room again, but still no Max McKenny. She wished she knew what excuse he had used because she'd sure like to try it out herself. She hated this blasted tea.

Then she turned back to Dexter and fixed him with her inquisitorial look. "So, Dex, why are you devoted to saving the wolves?"

The question seemed to startle him and he blinked rapidly. "Because they're an important part of the ecology."

She nodded. "Very true. I know a lot of people who just like them because they look like puppies."

"That's absurd. They're not domestic dogs. You couldn't bring one home with you. But they improve the ecology."

"I know. I've read about it. I just wondered if there was some special reason you took up the cause."

"It's what's good for the environment, that's all."

Which told her she was now going to be badgered by Dex on every possible environmental issue. Inwardly she sighed. Ten years of training as a reporter had hardened her against taking sides. She could have been fired for taking sides even on her personal time.

Well, she wasn't ready to take up any causes yet. She was still feeling too bruised by the loss of her beloved career. Too bruised by the failing newspaper industry that had made it impossible for her to find another job and necessary for her to teach when she'd rather do.

She was lucky, she told herself. A lot of her friends who had been laid off had had to leave journalism behind.

Just keep that in mind, she told herself as she eased

away from Dex and made her way to the door. *You're lucky. Even if you don't feel like you are.*

Summer warmth lingered, even with the earlier twilight and Liza chose to walk. Her apartment was only a few blocks away from the relatively new campus, and not too far from the semiconductor plant that had brought brief prosperity to the town before falling prey to an economic downswing and laying off about half its work force.

Most of those people had been forced to leave town, which meant the apartments were no longer full and rents had fallen. Given her salary as an adjunct, she supposed she should be grateful for that. But she really would have preferred living in the older part of town, seedy as some of it was, to living in the new sprawl that had been added over that past ten or so years.

Something had sure put her in a morose mood, she realized as she strode down sidewalks fronted by young trees. And here she thought she'd been getting over herself.

Maybe it wasn't so easy to lose a job you loved and then have to move halfway across the country for a new one, even if it was a matter of coming home. Except home had changed since she had left to go to college fourteen years ago. Some things looked the same, but they didn't feel the same.

You can never come home again. The old saying wafted through her mind and she decided it was true. The town had changed a bit, but so had she. And maybe the changes in her were the most momentous ones.

She sighed, the sound lost as the evening breeze ruffled the leaves of the scrawny little trees.

Well, at least there was now Max McKenny to

stretch her underworked brain muscles again. Her mind immediately served up another mental image of him, and she had to smother a smile lest she be seen walking all alone down the street, grinning like an idiot.

But she wanted to grin, for a variety of reasons. She'd seen how the girls went after an attractive teacher, and he was more attractive than most. Heck, she'd done a bit of it herself in college. All you had to do was stare intently, longingly, and you could fluster an inexperienced teacher. You didn't even have to follow them into their offices to rattle them and make them nervous. She wondered if Max had any idea what he might be in for being a new and interesting man in an area that didn't often see new guys.

She bit back a giggle.

Yup, he was in for it. And since she wasn't entirely immune herself, she would willingly bet he was going to have a lot to contend with.

Oh, he was yummy all right. She couldn't exactly put her finger on the reason. He was good-looking enough, but not star quality. No, it was more that he projected some kind of aura, the way he stood, a man supremely confident in his manhood, she guessed. No apologies there. Yet he hadn't struck her as cocky, which made him all the better.

She hated cocky men. She'd had too many cocky editors and interviewed too many cocky politicians.

So that was a definite mark in his favor. He'd been pleasant enough, and friendly enough. Polite. Respectful.

And oh so unrevealing.

That part she didn't like. Quickening her pace, she reached her building and trotted up the stairs. Her computer was still on, and she dropped her keys on the table as she hurried to it.

She wished she had all the resources she had once had as a reporter. But at least she had enough to begin her search into his background.

She started at the college's website, knowing they had to say at least something about his qualifications.

Maxwell McKenny, adjunct instructor, criminology. B.S. University of Michigan, J.D. Stetson University College of Law. Eight years law enforcement experience.

Good heavens, he had a law degree? A beat cop with a law degree? What in the world was he doing here in the back of nowhere? With that Juris Doctor degree he shouldn't have wound up teaching at a minuscule junior college in Wyoming.

And Stetson was in Florida, her old stomping grounds. He couldn't have gotten that degree while working for any Michigan police department. Which must mean he'd gotten it before he went to work as a cop, or after he had quit.

And why, when she had told him she'd worked as a reporter in Florida, hadn't he made the natural comment that he'd gone to law school there?

Because he had indeed been deflecting her.

Her nose twitched and her curiosity rose to new heights. Leaning forward again, she began a search of the American Bar Association. If he'd been admitted to the bar, he should be there somewhere.

"I'm going to find out who you are, Max," she muttered as she began her searches.

Because something is smelling like three-day-old fish.

Max rode back to the La-Z-Rest motel on his Harley, a hog he enjoyed immensely as the weather allowed and had missed during his last assignment. Soon he was going to have to find some old beater to get him through the winter, but for now he was free to enjoy the sensation of huge power beneath him and little to slow him down on the road. Not that he sped. He did nothing to draw unnecessary attention.

Although he'd evidently gotten the attention of Liza Enders, former journalist. Just what he needed: a reporter interested in him. Being noticed was anathema, and something he was trying very hard to avoid right now.

Then that temptress with the cat-green eyes had come striding across the room, and he'd stood there like a starstruck kid when he should have ducked, watching her rounded hips move, noticing her nicely sized breasts, drinking in her shiny, long auburn hair.

Idiot. He should have moved away the instant he realized she had focused on him. But how was he supposed to have guessed she was a reporter? All he'd noticed was that the loveliest faculty member in the room was walking his way.

Thinking with his small head, he thought disgustedly as he roared into the parking slot in front of his room. Responding with his gonads. He never did that. Not anymore.

It was too dangerous.

Frustrated with himself, he turned off the ignition, dismounted and kicked the stand into place. He gave the hog a pat then headed into his room.

Once there, he flopped on his back on the bed and clasped his hands behind his head. On the ceiling above him was a water spot that looked pretty much like the state of Texas.

He played over the conversation in his mind again,

recalling everything he had told her. Not much. That and the brief CV the college printed wouldn't really tell her a thing.

Well, except for that freaking law degree. She would probably find that odd for a beat cop, but he couldn't be the only one who had a J.D. So what if the reporter dug a little more? What would she find?

Very little. He wasn't even using his real name, not that that would make a difference. He'd gone so far to ground that even his real name wouldn't yield anything except possibly a birth date.

He was a man who didn't exist. And it had to stay that way for a while yet.

So why the hell had he allowed himself to be blinded by a pretty face and a luscious figure into holding still long enough to have a conversation? She'd been trying to get information about him. He was smart enough to know that. Many had tried over the years.

But maybe her curiosity was just passing. Maybe she'd let it go.

He'd have to keep an eye on her, that was for sure. If she started prying too much, he would have to hit the road. Not that he wanted to. He kind of liked the gig they'd set him up with here, in a place where you could spot a stranger from a hundred miles.

He kind of liked the thought of teaching. And even though he'd been here for only a short while, he kind of liked this town, too.

Finally he pulled his cell phone out of its holster and punched a number he tried not to call too often. One he definitely never put on speed dial and always erased from the phone's memory of recent calls.

"Ames here," said a familiar voice.

"Max."

"Oh, man, what's wrong?"

"I'm not sure. I just got the inquisition from a reporter. Are you sure my background holds up?"

"Considering how many databases we had to modify, yeah. It had better."

"A J.D. looks pretty funny hanging off a beat cop."

"Not if that cop wants to be a detective someday. Or run for prosecutor. Or teach at a college. Take your pick."

Max sighed and ran an impatient hand through his hair. "Okay."

"Why? Did she say she was going to check into you?"

"No, but her eyes did."

Ames surprised him with a laugh. "She must be pretty."

"You could say that. Why?"

"You noticed her eyes. Okay, we'll keep tabs on it. What's her name?"

"Liza Enders."

"Got it. What paper is she with?"

"None. She teaches at the college, too."

"All right. I'll blow the whistle if anything looks suspicious. In the meantime, I think one of our nerds can make sure she runs around the maypole a few times if she tries to crack your background."

"Thanks, buddy."

"That's what I'm here for. Need anything else?"

"No, that was it."

He put the phone away and resumed his contemplation of the ceiling. It wasn't long, though, before he was seeing Liza Enders rather than the Texas water spot.

She sure was an attractive armful. He didn't go for

the skinny women who looked more like boys, and no one would mistake Liza Enders for a boy.

She might be a great reporter, but he was better at a far more dangerous game. He knew from long experience how to cover his butt. And there was entirely too much at stake to let a reporter blow it.

His life, for one thing. And the lives of other innocents, too. Not to mention if he let anyone close to him, they could get caught in the cross fire.

He had to find a way to keep her distant.

He closed his eyes. At least it was safe to fantasize about her. It would never be more than that, but he'd been living on fantasies for a long time.

One more surely wouldn't hurt.

Growing hot and heavy, he imagined removing the clothes from Liza's curvy body.

Nope, it couldn't hurt.

He awoke in a cold sweat and sat bolt upright with his heart pounding. The room was dark except for a nervous strip of blinking red neon light that crept between the curtains.

For an instant he couldn't remember where he was. For an instant he wondered if someone had entered the room while he slept.

Reaching out, he found the pistol on his bedside table and thumbed off the safety. Was someone in the room with him? He listened, but heard nothing except the whine of truck tires on the state highway outside.

At last he flipped on the bedside light. Empty. Shoving himself off the bed he checked the tiny bathroom. He was all alone, the door still locked.

Sitting on the edge of the bed, pistol still in hand, he

waited for the adrenaline to wash away. Nightmares. He'd had a few of them in his time.

Dimly he remembered some of it. They'd found him. Yes, that was it. They'd found him. They surrounded him and threatened him and kept demanding his real name.

He hadn't been able to remember it. And each time he failed, they hit him again. It may have been a dream, but his head and stomach felt as if those blows had been real.

And Liza. She'd been there, too, demanding his identity.

As if he had one anymore.

Crap. He thumbed the safety on again and put the pistol on the table. Now he felt cold from the sweat drenching. He needed a shower, but didn't feel safe enough to take one. Not yet.

That damn reporter was going to be a problem. He had to get rid of her somehow.

This might look like a game to her, but for him it was life or death.

Chapter 2

By morning, Liza's curiosity had only grown. Max McKenny had indeed graduated from the University of Michigan and Stetson College of Law, both with high honors. Beyond that, she hadn't found a thing, even when she searched Michigan newspapers for his name, thinking he might have been on a case that had gotten some publicity.

But responding cops seldom made the news unless something spectacular came down. Unless a cop was involved in a shoot-out or something equally serious, only the Public Information Officer talked to the press, rarely mentioning the specific cops involved. Very often the names of the first responders never rose to the surface of awareness. So Max might just have had a dull career.

The lack of information wasn't terribly surprising, except that there was no record at all of any Maxwell

McKennys in Michigan. It wasn't a common name, and that should have made her job easier. Instead, her search was giving her a blank wall.

The American Bar Association had proved opaque. If it had a public membership directory, it wasn't available online. Checking state licensing boards, as she'd learned long ago, was a total wash if you didn't get the name exactly right. Maxwell McKenny, if listed as Maxwell D. McKenny, would never show up in a search.

Ah, well.

She tried to force her attention back to the day's work ahead and forget she'd awakened from a dream that morning about a gorgeous hunk of manhood who resembled Max. Not entirely, but close enough that she couldn't fool her waking brain into thinking it had just been a generalized dream.

Maybe part of her problem was that it had been way too long since she'd had a boyfriend, something which had everything to do with her former career. There were just so many times you could break a date before a guy went looking elsewhere. Which pretty much meant she had to date other reporters who would understand her schedule, except most of the single men in her newsroom just hadn't appealed to her. There had been one guy—but she cut that thought off with a scythe. She was not going there.

So maybe she was just focusing on Max because a hunk had walked into view. Maybe this was all some kind of female reaction and not her nose for news at all.

A Harley roared by her as she strode down the sidewalk toward campus, and even from the back she could see it was Max, helmet notwithstanding. Of course.

He would have a Harley, big and black, a machine that throbbed with energy and a deep-throated roar. It fit.

Hadn't she read somewhere that motorcycle cops had thrown fits in some state when officials had wanted to replace their Harleys with something less expensive? Apparently other motorcycles just didn't sound as good.

Or something. That had been a long time ago, and she couldn't even remember where she'd read it. Maybe Max had been a motorcycle cop. That would have made his life more boring than most, though handing out traffic tickets was one of the most dangerous jobs cops faced. Even so, most motorcycle cops never ran into any real trouble.

And almost none of them made the news.

She shook her head at herself, deciding she was probably making a mountain out of a molehill. It wasn't as if her instincts were infallible. She could be very wrong about this.

Much to her amazement, the Harley stopped at the corner and pulled a U-turn, coming back to idle beside her. "Want a lift?" Max asked as he raised the smoky visor that concealed his face.

She was tempted to tell him no, that she enjoyed walking on such a lovely morning, and that would have been true. But equally true was the fact that she hadn't been on a motorcycle since her college days, and she'd liked it back then. It was tempting.

Even more tempting was wrapping her arms around his waist and discovering if his stomach was as hard and flat as it had looked in that T-shirt. Having her legs extended around his.

Was she losing her mind? Common sense reared. "Thanks," she said, "but no helmet."

He flipped open a steel compartment on the side of

the hog and pulled one out. "I always carry an extra." Reaching out, he strapped it to her head, securing it beneath her chin. "You done this before?"

"A long, long time ago." Part of her wanted to rebel at the way he was taking charge, but another, stronger part of her really wanted to ride behind him on that bike.

So he guided her onto the seat behind him, warning her about the exhaust pipes, and helped her place her feet properly.

"Lean with me," he reminded her, and then she was sailing toward the school with her arms and legs wrapped around him, thinking how envious all those young girls were going to be when they saw this.

The thought startled her, it was so juvenile, and she laughed out loud at herself.

"It's fun, isn't it," his muffled voice said, misunderstanding the source of her laughter. There was certainly no reason to tell him the truth.

Well, she could now testify that his stomach was hard and flat beneath the leather jacket, and the thighs she was pressed against were every bit as hard. Being wrapped around him this way was causing a deep throbbing in her center.

Oh, man, she had it bad. The bug had bitten. Knowing not one thing about him, really, she wanted to have sex with him. Shouldn't she have outgrown that a long time ago?

All too soon he pulled them into a faculty parking slot, and seconds later the engine's roar choked off.

"Wow," she said. "I haven't done that in so long."

"Maybe one Saturday before the weather turns cold I'll take her out on the mountain roads," he said easily. "I'll bet it's beautiful up there."

"Right now especially."

He twisted, offering one arm to help her lever herself off the bike. She was honestly sorry when her feet hit firm ground again. Reluctantly, she reached up to unsnap the helmet.

"That was awesome," she admitted as she handed the helmet back, then watched him stow it. "Thanks."

"My pleasure." He pulled his own helmet off and hesitated. "Maybe, if you want, you could take that mountain ride with me."

It was her turn to hesitate. The ride sounded like incredible fun, but she still couldn't escape that strange feeling about him. "I don't know anything about you," she said finally.

His polar-ice eyes narrowed a hair, then he surprised her by laughing. "Of course you don't. We just met. Do you want my fingerprints and birth certificate first?"

All of a sudden she felt foolish for her suspicions. "No, of course not."

He leaned toward her a little, his teeth still gleaming in a smile. "Getting to know each other takes time, Liza. Don't you think?"

Then he hopped off the bike, waved and headed to his class.

She stood there feeling utterly flat-footed. How had he done that? He'd told her exactly not one thing more about himself yet had managed to make her feel foolish for even wondering.

Yet, she argued with herself, he was right. It took time to get to know someone personally. But she was still annoyed by the feeling that he was deflecting her.

Why should he? Surely the college wouldn't have hired someone with a criminal record. They did background checks as well she knew. So why couldn't she be satisfied with just knowing that he was another instructor like her? Exactly like her.

Because something about him seemed different? Because something didn't feel quite right?

Sheesh. Shouldering her backpack, she started the short hike to her office. She hated questioning her own instincts, but maybe it was time to start. She was rusty, and even when she hadn't been rusty she'd made an occasional mistake.

Well, she thought they were occasional mistakes only because she hadn't come up with anything about the person who aroused her suspicions. That didn't exactly mean those persons were okay.

When she reached her office, she tossed her bag on her desk and powered up her computer. She needed to check the presentation for her first class, a comparison between a TV news story and the actual facts of a legal case that showed how easily a reporter could create a false impression. It was important to her that her students understood exactly how the news could be bent before they got into the nitty-gritty of trying to write it.

Maybe she was getting a false impression now. Maybe Max was nobody at all but a former cop with a law degree who had decided to take a break by teaching at a community college. Maybe all her questions arose from the simple fact that he seemed out of place here.

It could all be as simple as that. As simple as her training driving her to look for the story behind the story, even if there wasn't one. Man, no wonder guys didn't much hang out with her. Not only had she worked weird hours, but dating her must have been like dating an inquisitor, now that she thought about it.

Few answers were good enough for her. She always wanted more information.

All of a sudden she remembered a boyfriend from five years ago who had erupted at her. "I can't just say it's a nice day," he had snapped. "You always want to know exactly what kind of nice day it is. Did something good happen? What's the temperature? Can I tell you the exact color blue of the sky?"

She winced at the memory, mostly because there was more than a kernel of truth to it.

She had defended herself by demanding to know what was wrong with curiosity. She still believed there was nothing wrong with it, but maybe she was just too impatient for the answers. She'd give Max some time, she decided. If she kept getting the feeling he was too much of a mystery, then she could start digging.

She wondered how long she'd be able to rein herself in.

She learned the answer not two minutes later when she realized she was researching active law licenses in the state of Michigan.

She had it bad.

Max strolled to his office, wondering if he'd done the right thing in stopping to pick up Liza and offering her a trip into the mountains.

Yes, he decided. One of the things he had learned quickly was not to act suspiciously, and one of the most suspicious things you could do was avoid someone who was asking questions about you.

The only way to seem aboveboard was to act as if you were. And while he was at it, maybe he could convince her that she really didn't want to know him or know more about him. Given his job, he knew how to be obnoxiously overbearing, and with an independent woman like Liza, that might be just the ticket.

He tossed his helmet on the desk and brought his computer up. He had some idea how to teach the course he was about to begin. It hadn't been that long since he'd taken such a course himself, and he knew that part of what students would want to hear were actual on-the-job experiences. He'd heard enough stories to tell them as if they were his own.

He'd even managed to rustle up his own course outline and enough handouts to get him rolling. He figured he could pull this off as well as any role he'd ever had to play. And unlike Liza Enders, his students weren't going to be suspicious.

Nope, the teaching part would be a walk in the park compared to some of the stuff he'd had to do—like lie.

There were some folks who deserved to be lied to. And then there were the rest, who didn't deserve it at all.

What was that old joke? The drug dealer is more honest than the average narc, because the narc lies about what he is.

The thought made him shift uncomfortably in his seat.

Keep your eye on the ball, he reminded himself. It was a familiar refrain in his life. He had to keep his eye on the ball here, an important ball. And that was definitely going to mean keeping an eye on Liza Enders.

There were worse jobs, he decided. But nothing that began with a lie could end well. In fact, lies usually just blew up on you.

And right now, he wondered if Liza Enders was going to wind up being a grenade.

* * *

Two days later, Liza sat in the back of her own classroom, listening as Sheriff Gage Dalton explained why cops used Public Information Officers to speak with the press. But her mind was elsewhere.

She'd learned that Max did indeed have an active law license in Michigan, but no address for a practice. Private addresses were confidential. Okay, he was licensed. That part of his CV was real. But she had learned absolutely not one more thing, and that bothered her.

Gage, a former DEA agent, a man with a limp and a face badly scarred from burns received from a car bomb that had killed his first family, looked comfortable in front of the class explaining matters.

"You've got to understand why we need to control information flow," he said. "First off, ongoing investigations need to be protected. We can't share information that might tip off a criminal to how much we know. We can't share information that might implicate someone who is innocent. We can't share anything we're not a hundred percent certain of. So we have a spokesperson who knows exactly what we can and cannot say."

She nodded to herself, understanding it only too well, although it had caused her a lot of frustration during her years on the crime beat.

He went into some detail about the Atlanta Olympics bombing and how he felt that had been mishandled. Pencils and pens were scrabbling quickly across notepaper, fingers were typing rapidly on laptops as the students listened, enthralled.

Finally Gage looked at her. "Do you have anything to add, Ms. Enders?"

She smiled and stood up. "Of course I do. It's still

my job as a reporter to get everything out of you and any other source I can find and report it. So, class, you could say we have an adversarial relationship here. There's a fine line between respecting an investigation and buying public statements hook, line and sinker."

Gage nodded agreement. "Sometimes the press can be really helpful to us. Other times they can cause problems."

The two of them batted stories back and forth and answered students' questions until the class ended. Gage remained until the last student left, then he turned to Liza.

"I haven't told you yet, but it's good to have you back in town."

"I haven't been back that long and you hardly knew me before I left."

He winked. "But I'm sure you knew me."

"Oh, everyone knew who you were."

"Hell's own archangel," he said.

She almost gasped. "You heard that?"

"Everything gets around this town sooner or later. I can't say I blame anyone for calling me that. I came out of nowhere with death in my eye, I suppose."

"But no one thinks of you that way anymore," she assured him.

"No, probably not anymore."

She hesitated. "Say, Gage?"

"Yes?"

"Do you know Max McKenny?"

Cops were good, especially cops like Gage, who'd worked undercover, but she caught an instant of stillness before he responded. "Only that he asked me to talk to one of his classes, too."

"Yeah? About what?"

"My undercover days and how you have to work to stay inside the law when you're trying to get in with people who are constantly breaking it."

"That's a good topic," she admitted. "You were DEA, right?"

He nodded. "And I had to get through it without ever doing drugs myself. It's not easy, and it can cause a lot of suspicion. Why do you want to know about Mc-Kenny?"

"I don't know a damn thing about him," she said frankly. "Something doesn't add up."

"Such as?"

"I can't exactly put my finger on it. He wants to take me up into the mountains on a ride sometime."

Gage shook his head. "You reporters. I did his background check for the college, Liza. Is that good enough?"

She felt like squirming, wondering yet again if she was being unreasonable about all this. Maybe this was nothing but a major fail for her instincts. Or maybe her whole problem with Max was that she was nervous about the attraction she felt for him. Attraction had given her nothing but grief in her past.

"I guess it's good enough," she said finally to Gage. "He's clean?"

"They hired him, didn't they?" Gage smiled that crooked smile of his and headed for the door. "Let me know if he does anything to justify your suspicion."

Ouch, she said to herself as Gage disappeared.

She thought again about the complaint her ex-boyfriend had made. Was she really too inquisitive? Too suspicious? Maybe so, she admitted as she returned to her office. Max McKenny had passed a background check performed by the sheriff's office. That should be enough for her. Absolutely enough.

His reasons for coming here to teach were purely personal and none of her business unless he made it hers. God, she needed to rein this in. Even Gage thought she was being a bit ridiculous, although he hadn't come right out and said so.

She was walking head down, waging an internal war with herself as she crossed the quadrangle. A few dead leaves rustled as they blew by her, an early announcement of autumn, but she barely noticed them.

Okay, she was trained to want to know everything, but she wasn't trained to question everyone who crossed her path. What had Max done to arouse her suspicion except seem out of place? And who was she to decide he was out of place?

Heck, she was out of place herself.

So a good-looking guy with a law enforcement background came all the way from Michigan to teach at an out-of-the-way junior college. Maybe it was the only job he could find, given that jobs were harder to find than ladybugs without spots. She ought to know that, since she'd spent months searching after she got her pink slip.

Maybe he really did just want a break from chasing speeders. He wouldn't be the first cop who found the job not to his taste after a while.

And look at her. If her life had followed her plan, she'd be working at an even bigger daily paper now instead of teaching.

She sighed.

Okay, maybe all this was happening simply because she was frightened of being so attracted to him. Maybe she was doing the deflecting, finding reasons to try to stomp down that attraction. Any other woman with these feelings would be trying to draw Max's attention, not trying to find something unsavory in his past.

Maybe years as a reporter had screwed up her thinking in some major way. It had certainly screwed up her life and her relationships with men.

Just as she was concluding that this was all about scars from old relationships and fears of garnering new ones, she saw the booted feet in front of her.

Too late to stop, she collided with Max McKenny's hard body. At once he gripped her elbows and steadied her.

"Oops," she said and looked up reluctantly. To her horror a blush heated her cheeks, as if he could read every thought in her head. Not to mention her lack of attention that had caused the collision.

"Sorry," he said. "Are you all right? I wasn't paying close enough attention."

Another ouch. If her head had been up, she wouldn't have been able to avoid seeing him approach. She would have fixated on it. But he hadn't even noticed her.

"I'm fine," she said in a muffled voice, embarrassment and annoyance both rising in her.

"One of my students called to me," he offered pleasantly enough as he released her elbows. "Note to self, never turn head while walking forward."

The heat began to leave her cheeks. "I could give myself the same note."

"You were lost in thought. Your head was down. I should have kept that in mind."

"I shouldn't walk when I'm woolgathering," she admitted, stepping back a little when all she wanted to do was step forward and press herself up against him. Her cheeks warmed again. "Sorry."

"Hey, we teach at a college. Aren't we supposed to be absentminded?"

That smile again, that devastating smile. It reached out and filled her with warmth, especially in her most secret places. God, she hoped he couldn't smell her pheromones. She was glad when the breeze quickened, blowing any possibility away. "I don't think we're supposed to be that absentminded," she replied.

He laughed quietly. "I was coming to look for you."

Her heart leaped and she forced it back down. "But my office is that way." She pointed.

"I checked your schedule and figured you were on your way back from class."

Another wave of heat rolled through her. She almost hated him for the effect he had on her. "Oh," she said, unable to think of anything witty. "Why?"

"Because tomorrow's Saturday. It's going to be a beautiful day. Want to ride up into the mountains with me?"

She wanted to say no just because she wasn't ready to admit she might be a fool. Because she really didn't trust men all that much. Because it would be easier to convince herself all over again that this man had something to hide than it would be to risk the possibility of getting hurt by him.

But Gage's reassurance rang in her ears, reminding her that she'd never vetted a boyfriend before. Besides, this was a bike ride, not a date. He probably thought it would be more fun to share the time than ride alone.

And she really, really wanted to go. She knew she was lying to herself when she decided it would be an opportunity to learn more about him. She just wanted to be on that bike, wrapped around him, winding up mountain roads with the wind in her face and the changing leaves showing between the firs.

"Yes," she said, the word escaping her before she even realized it was coming.

"Great." His smile widened a bit. "I'll pick you up around ten, so the air has a chance to warm."

She gave him directions to her apartment building, promising to be out front.

"Wear something warm and rugged," he said. "Basic safety rule."

"I know. Thanks."

Then before she could gather herself, he was striding away again.

She realized that she watched Max walk away an awful lot for someone she had just met.

Resuming her trek to her office, not all that far really given the small size of the campus, she wondered if she needed her head examined.

She only wished she knew who was crazier, Liza the woman or Liza the reporter. At the moment, it seemed like a toss-up.

Hiding in plain sight is how Max explained it to himself. The best way to defang Liza's suspicions was to make himself available as if he had not a single thing to hide. It had always worked before.

Besides, riding on the bike wouldn't provide a whole lot of opportunities for in-depth questions or conversations. Of course, he was planning to bring a picnic lunch for them to enjoy, but that was part of the illusion.

Because he was all illusion. Sometimes he wondered if any part of his real self still existed. Every so often, the question would rise up and sting him.

Who was he? Damned if he really knew anymore.

Doing his job required learning to think like the people he associated with. He not only had to reflect their actions, but also their thoughts so he would never slip, never be caught unawares, never give himself away.

Maybe he was just questioning himself because he'd been dumped into a new role and still hadn't learned to entirely think the part. Worse, this role was only temporary, so part of him was resisting the change.

It was, he vowed, going to be his last game. He was going to finish this and then try to find his way back to who he really was before his thinking got so messed up he needed a decade on an analyst's couch.

Easy to think, maybe not so easy to do. Sometimes he honestly wondered.

Late that night, he got on his bike and roared along the back roads of Conrad County. He had a contact here—a name given to him by Ames—who he could turn to if he needed to. But existential questions weren't exactly the kind of thing he was supposed to need help with.

No, he was left with his own personality disarray and his own questions to be dealt with as he wrapped up his final job.

So what exactly did he know that was real? The bike between his legs, the almost-crazy ride down dark county roads and Liza.

His thoughts persistently came back to Liza. She was real. He wasn't so sure, though, about how he was responding to her. Yes, she was acting on him like a sexual magnet, but she wasn't the first, nor would she be the last, probably.

No, there was something else about her. Something that suggested her greatest lust was for truth, one lust he wouldn't be able to satisfy.

He'd had some problems with his job before, times when he had questioned himself, but never before had he felt soiled by it.

Until now. Thanks to her.

His motives didn't matter, not a bit.

How was he supposed to deal with that?

By playing the game out, he realized as he twisted the throttle up until he was tearing down the road like a bat out of hell. By playing it out.

He had no other choice.

Far, far away in a run-down section of Washington, D.C., a woman with long black hair and a sequined tube dress beneath a baggy olive drab jacket walked swiftly along dangerous streets with loudly tapping heels. More than once a car pulled up to the curb, but when the driver rolled down the passenger window to accost her, she shot him a death look that made him peel away fast. In her pocket, she clutched a small pistol, and each time her hand tightened around it.

She made it back to the abandoned, derelict apartment house, the one with the big signs saying it was scheduled for demolition, and slipped in through a back way until she reached an apartment in the middle of the hall.

She stepped into a filthy room where a bunch of mattresses padded the floor. A kerosene heater fought off the night's chill.

Five men waited for her, all of them dressed in various kinds of cast-off army-style clothing. She couldn't have looked more out of place.

They all looked up at her arrival.

"I got his real name," she said with savage pride. "It was like we thought. And if that isn't enough, I've got a date with the source in two nights. The way this guy is crumbling, I'll probably get an address pretty soon."

The man who went by the name Jody sat bolt upright. "Give me the name. I'll find the bastard no matter where he's hiding."

The woman smiled, and it wasn't pleasant. "Maybe you can. But if you can't, I will." She fingered the switchblade in her other pocket. She did like to use a knife, and a certain ATF agent was going to be her next work of art.

Chapter 3

Max was waiting for Liza when she emerged from her apartment building into bright autumn sunshine. He stood leaning against his silent bike, his arms folded, clad head to toe in leathers for the road.

Max wore "bad boy biker" pretty well, she had to admit.

She herself wore her thickest jeans and heaviest boots, and a sweater beneath a ripstop nylon jacket. Not nearly as good as leathers, but she didn't have the money or the ability to buy leathers overnight.

She noticed that Max had added a backrest to the pillion seat for her. A thoughtful gesture, one she certainly hadn't expected.

He greeted her with a smile and held a helmet out to her. "I was half convinced you wouldn't show."

"I don't do that," she said, although she could have admitted with equal honesty that if she'd had his number she might have called him any of a half-dozen times the night before to cancel. As many times as she'd been obliged to break a date, never had she failed to call. Maybe lacking his personal phone number was the only reason she was out here right now.

No, said a merciless voice in her mind. *Quit playing games with yourself.* She was out here because she wanted to spend time with Max, to ride that Harley, clinging to him and see what came next. Despite all her fears of rejection, she still couldn't resist.

She was feeling a sense of adventure unlike any she'd known in a long time. The thrill of taking a risk. Ready to cast caution to the winds, to go along for the ride, sure that it would at least be exciting.

Lately she'd felt she was in danger of getting stodgy. No way was she going to let that happen.

So she let the excitement of the moment take her, and she mounted the bike behind Max. With the backrest, she didn't necessarily need to cling to him as closely, but she clung anyway, her head pressed to his leather-covered back, her cheek liking the feel of that leather as she watched the world whip past sideways.

In fact, she liked it so much that not until she began to feel a bit dizzy did she lift her head to look forward at the ribbon of rising road. The height of the pillion gave her the ability to look right over Max's shoulder as they started their climb into the mountains.

With increasing altitude, the color of the leaves brightened, dotting the mostly evergreen forest with blotches of orange and gold. The air also grew colder and she wished she had put on her gloves.

Each time they rounded a bend, her thighs tightened around Max as she leaned with him, and she was getting so aroused that she started to lose track of the passing world. The rumble of the bike itself only added to her heightened awareness and as the miles passed, she gave in to it.

Why not? He'd never know.

She began to wonder what would happen if they stopped. Was he feeling the same way? Possibly. If he was, what if he reached out for her, took her without warning or preamble?

She rather liked that idea. Talking only got in the way sometimes, and her body was awakening in a way that suggested being dragged off to a cave by her hair might be the perfect outcome.

She laughed silently into the wind, amused by the turn of her thoughts even as they continued to wash over her with increasingly blatant visions.

Yeah, he could just pull her off the bike when they stopped, and toss her on the ground—pine needles and leaves would probably make a soft enough bed, although the practical reporter in her was sure there'd be a rock in exactly the wrong place. Then he'd slip his hands, probably chilly, up under her sweater and…

Her thighs clamped around his in response. Thank goodness he didn't have eyes in the back of his head because she was sure she'd turned beet red when she realized what she had done.

"Okay back there?" he called.

"Fine," she lied. If fine was feeling like a stew pot that had suddenly been turned on high and wanted to boil over.

"I want to stop at the old mining town up ahead."

"Okay," she agreed as loudly as she could manage when it was impossible to breathe. Sheesh, the guy hadn't done one suggestive thing and she was already on her way to bed with him.

No way.

He pulled off the road a half mile farther along and slowed as they started down a bumpy rutted old wagon track. She recognized it from her high school days but was surprised he knew it was here.

"How'd you know about this?" she asked.

"One of the faculty told me. Said I couldn't miss it."

"You can't if you know what it is," she agreed, her voice bobbling as the bike bounced hard.

"Sorry," he said, and slowed even more.

Another half mile and they emerged into the area surrounding the old mining town. Signs, rusting a bit, warned them not to get any closer to the tumbledown buildings. The ground was pitted in a few places from cave-ins.

Max halted the bike, though the engine still rumbled. "Is it really that unsafe?"

"Very," she said. "The ground all around is honeycombed with old shafts. Nobody knows how long they'll hold out or exactly where they are."

"I vote for using my good sense then." He switched off the ignition, put down the stand, then slid off the bike with amazing ease. Turning, he helped her to the ground.

For an instant she thought her legs were going to give out. She must have been clinging to him tighter than she had realized, and the vibration of the bike had become so familiar her body wasn't ready to recognize it was gone.

He pulled off his leather gloves, shoved them into the pockets of his jacket, then reached for her hands. "Sorry I didn't think about this," he said.

"About what?"

"How cold you were likely to get without gloves." A

faint smile accompanied the words as he sandwiched her hands between both of his large ones. He rubbed her flesh briskly, warming it.

"I'm too used to Florida," she mumbled. "I have gloves. Silly me, I tucked them in my pockets instead of putting them on."

His chuckle was warm, and regret filled her when he let go of her hands.

He turned to face the ramshackle town, a place full of the remnants of old buildings, silvered by the years. "The kid in me really wants to explore."

"I know. I did when I was young and foolish."

"But how come nothing is growing?" he asked, indicating the clearing around the town. It was actually quite huge, extending in an oval that looked as if the ground had recently been cleared.

"Tailings from the mines," she said. "They were removed maybe fifteen years ago because they contained so many heavy metals. Poisonous stuff, and it was getting into the groundwater."

"What kind of poisonous stuff?"

"Uranium for one thing. Some of that ground is still radioactive, and nothing grows on it. Then there's arsenic, lead, zinc, bunches of stuff."

"How radioactive is it?"

"Probably not that bad or we wouldn't be allowed to get even this close."

"I guess." He looked at her. "How did you learn all that?"

"There was a lot of discussion when they wanted to clean it up, and I did a little research on my own."

"Always the reporter, huh?"

She didn't know whether to smile or frown. "Some things are ingrained."

"Well, natural caution suggests this wouldn't be a great place for our picnic. But I would like to look around a bit before we find a better spot."

A picnic? She hadn't expected that, and the thought delighted her. Clearly he was in no hurry to take her back. Feeling lighter, she walked around the edge of the clearing with him.

"This is fascinating," he said as they paused to look at the small town from a different angle. "Imagine how hard folks must have worked up here to dig all these mines. What were they looking for?"

"Gold. It played out fast from what I hear. You can find isolated mines all over the mountain, though. They're all barred up now."

He nodded. "I don't think any sensible person would want to risk their necks in one of them. Timbers must have rotted. Water may have destabilized the ground."

"Obviously. Look at the cave-ins. So far they've been in areas where the mines are shallower, but can you imagine how deep some of these must go? And back when the tailings piles were here, you could really see how hard those guys worked. Huge mounds of broken rock, all pulled out of the ground with a bucket, a pulley and maybe a mule."

"I'm almost sorry they cleaned it up."

"You can see pictures of it in the library. But I know what you mean. When they took the tailings, they took away history. All sense of what this place used to be. Now it could be almost any old ghost town." Her eyes were drawn to a bit of faded cloth flapping in a window. Somebody's curtain from over a century ago hadn't quite rotted. "Evidently in its day it was a pretty wild place. No law, claim jumping, a few murders. A saloon that collapsed years ago. Just imagine, men brought their families to a place like this."

He nodded, studying the town. "Everybody was hoping to strike it rich and then get the hell out of here, I suppose."

That surprised a laugh from her. "I guess so. I hadn't thought of that. It never became big and grand like some mining towns, so there wouldn't be much to hold anyone here except a hope and a prayer. A very basic, very difficult life."

"And what about Conard City? Did that come before or after?"

"About the same time, actually. Cattle ranching was already underway, as I recall, when they found gold up here. And with those big ranches, you still needed a town for other things. Some central location for a blacksmith, a church or two—"

"And don't forget bars. I can't imagine cowboys without bars."

"When I was a kid I saw the tail end of that. They'd come to town on Friday nights with their pay, and for a little while the cops were very busy, although they tried to look the other way. I hear it was even rougher when my parents were kids. Rougher but contained, the way they told it. My mother joked that she never needed a calendar to know when the weekend came. The streets filled up with pickup trucks."

"It seems like a quiet town now."

"It always mostly was, I guess. If you're interested in local history, you should talk to Miss Emma."

"Who's that?"

She looked at him and found him looking right back at her. Those polar-ice eyes snatched her breath away. There was a noticeable pause before she answered.

"Emmaline Dalton. Everyone calls her Miss Emma, although I don't know why. Anyway, she's the librarian, and her family was one of the very first to settle here. Her father was a judge, so she probably has lots of interesting stories apart from the library archives."

"Dalton? Any relation to the sheriff?"

"His wife."

"Ah."

He nodded, glanced back to the town. "Well, since we can't safely explore, I guess it's time to move on and find a good place for a chilly picnic."

This time when they mounted the bike she put her gloves on. It didn't matter. He grabbed her hands and tucked them up inside his leather jacket. Warmth from his body, and a marvelous sense of intimacy filled her. Even through her gloves she could feel hard, rippling muscles as they bounced back down the rutted track to the paved road.

"So where is it they want to put this new resort?" he shouted over the bike's roar.

"Just up ahead about two miles."

When they reached the pavement's end, he pulled them off into a small glade where a few late wildflowers blossomed in red and gold. The air smelled so fresh up here, scented with pine and mulch, and the trees were close enough to swallow the breeze. A few deciduous trees edged the small glade, their leaves like golden teardrops.

The cloudless day was so beautiful that she couldn't help but let go of all her curiosity and suspicion. Max was just another guy, albeit damned attractive, and there didn't seem to be one thing about him to arouse her curiosity. Not now, not today.

She was content to sit on the ground and lean back

against a log while he pulled out sandwiches and bot-
tles of water. She could tell by the packaging that he'd
picked up the sandwiches at Maude's diner, and her
mouth watered.

"So," he said, "this Dexter guy has been bearding
me about saving the wolves up here."

"He got me, too."

"Are there many of them?"

"There's a pack, maybe two. I guess all of a dozen
or so."

He nodded and settled beside her, also using the
fallen log as a backrest. "Down from Yellowstone?"

"They must be. There's no place else left for them
to come from."

"Is Dexter a pain in the butt?"

She grinned. "I don't know yet. I guess we'll find
out. So tell me, why aren't you practicing law? Isn't that
why most people get a law degree?"

"Most do, I suppose."

Biting into a sandwich helped her to remain silent
and wait for an explanation, but when it didn't come,
her suspicions about him rose to the fore again. "Is
there a reason," she asked when she finally swallowed,
"that you don't want to discuss it?"

He looked at her. "That's a helluva loaded question.
Sort of like, When did you stop beating your wife?"

She couldn't help laughing. "No, no, I didn't mean it
that way. I just wondered." Although truthfully, maybe
she had meant it that way. This guy kept making her
bristle with suspicion, no matter how ordinary he appeared. Instinct told her that meant he wasn't ordinary
and she'd better take care.

He shrugged, chewing a bite of sandwich before
answering. "I haven't made up my mind," he said fi-

nally. "The law fascinates me, obviously. That's why I became a cop, in part. But the longer I was a cop, the more I wanted to understand just what I was enforcing, and the more I realized I didn't want to be a cop forever. Studying law seemed like the way to go. Lots of opportunities. If I wanted, I could become a prosecutor, maybe. Work in a private practice. Get into politics. Teach."

"So now you're teaching. Do you like it?"

"It's early days yet. So far it's fun."

"I bet the girls are all over you," she said. She couldn't help it.

"You mean my students?" He lifted a brow. "Well, they do seem to cluster around a bit."

She snorted. "You're a new guy in a quiet town. Interesting. Attractive. I bet it's more like flies to a honey pot."

He unleashed a laugh. "Not yet, Liza. Not yet."

"It'll get there."

"Are you warning me to protect my chastity?"

She snickered. "Not exactly. I just remember being that age and how some interesting, attractive professor could rev me up. They'll swarm eventually."

"What revs you up now?"

The question caught her sideways, and she almost blurted the truth: you. Thank goodness for that small hesitation between brain and mouth.

"Curiosity?" he suggested smoothly. "Like wanting to know everything about someone new?"

"Not everything!"

He smiled. "Okay. How about the Cliff's Notes version. I was born in Michigan, after college I joined the...department, took some time to get my law degree, and otherwise I've been yawning a lot."

She wondered if that hesitation before department meant anything. She sat up a little straighter, but decided not to probe that. She didn't want to warn him he might have slipped because that usually turned people into clams. "No wife, no kids, no significant other?"

"Nope. Being on the streets only appeals to women until they have to live with it. It's stressful and I saw a lot of spouses leave because of it."

She nodded. "I saw that in my job, too. Bad hours. But your job had a lot of danger, as well."

"Some. But you can't blame a person for not wanting to wonder if someone they love is going to come home. Not everyone has a problem with it, but it takes a toll. I figured I'd wait until I changed careers."

"And here you are, with a brand-new career."

"That was the point." He returned to eating his sandwich.

She bit her lip, then said, "You went to Stetson College of Law, right?"

"Right."

"Then how come you didn't mention it when I said I'd been working for a paper in Florida?"

He turned slowly to look at her, and something in his gaze seemed to harden slightly, just a little, but enough to almost make her shiver. "It never occurred to me. Is it all that important that I was there for three years? I've lived other places, too."

She didn't know how to answer him. While most people would automatically have said, "I lived there for a while," when she mentioned Florida, that didn't mean everyone would.

She looked down at her sandwich. This guy was a cop. He was probably used to asking questions, not offering information.

So maybe this was an innocent difference in their way of making connections. She was a reporter who had spent a lot of years learning to create rapport. His job was different, and maybe had taught him different things.

Or maybe it was something else. Trying to explain it away wasn't making her feel any easier.

"I just thought it was curious, that's all," she said firmly, and bit into her sandwich to forestall any other questions. She had asked too many. How many times had she been told that she asked too many questions? More than she could count.

After a moment he spoke again. "I just didn't think about it, Liza. Everyone who looked at my CV knows I went to Stetson."

"True," she mumbled around a mouthful of food.

He put his sandwich down on the bag it had come in and rolled over on his hip, so he faced her directly. It was an open posture, almost welcoming. "I'm driving you nuts," he said. "I don't talk enough about myself."

Bingo, she thought.

"I'm not used to it," he said when she didn't reply. "I've never been terribly outgoing, most of my social life revolved around people I worked with, and I'm just not good at casual talk except the joking kind."

"Well, I can understand that, I guess. And I've been told often enough that I ask too many questions."

He gave her a crooked smile. "My sense of humor would probably appall most civilians."

At that she nodded and laughed. "I know the kind you mean. We shared it in the press room. We didn't dare tell those jokes to outsiders."

"Exactly."

"But that's how you deal with the ugliness," she

said presently. "With bad jokes about things that most people wouldn't find funny at all."

"Yeah. And there's a lot of ugliness."

She shook herself, realizing that she was in danger of leading them to discuss that stuff. A lot of which she had tried to forget. "Sorry. Let's move on, as they say."

For now, anyway. His momentary hesitation might mean nothing. And his explanations seemed valid. He was just a closemouthed man. He wasn't the first she'd ever met.

And it sounded like he'd seen enough ugliness himself. She had to admit there were parts of herself and her experience she had never shared with anyone.

She sighed and resumed eating. *Idiot,* she told herself. She was making up some kind of fantasy in her head, thinking she was going to uncover some great story.

Man, she wasn't even a reporter anymore, and he was just another teacher. A former cop with ugly stories in his background looking for a better life.

And if she was smart, she'd just let it lie, leave the man in peace and deal with the raging hormones that were probably the source of her feeling unsettled about him.

In fact, considering that hormones had caused her nothing but trouble, she'd be smart to clear out before this got any stickier and she wound up with a knife in her heart. Just move on, pretend he didn't exist. Life would be so much easier.

It sounded like a good plan. She wondered how long it would last.

The hardest part of packing up the picnic and taking Liza home, Max thought, was taking Liza home. Without finding out if her curves felt as good as he thought they would under his hands. Whether that inquisitive mouth of hers tasted as good as it looked.

But, he assured himself as they roared down the mountain, his mission was accomplished. He was fairly certain he had seemed open enough to reassure her, yet had responded in a way that would make her less likely to ask about him.

At least he hoped so. She had certainly seemed embarrassed for questioning him, yet her questions hadn't been truly out of line.

That was going to cause a problem, he realized. At some point she was going to stop feeling awkward about asking, and start wondering why ordinary questions were met with deflection and resistance.

Maybe he wasn't so bright after all.

Worse, he'd caught the flicker of attraction in her eyes along with the curiosity. He couldn't afford a relationship, not now, but he wasn't sure he would be able to avoid it.

Hell, he didn't even want to. Not this time. When he got her back to her apartment, what he most wanted to do was wrap her up in his arms and kiss her.

But he couldn't afford to nurture that flicker between them. So he waved goodbye and rode off.

As he headed back to the La-Z-Rest, something else occurred to him: if the people hunting him found him, Liza would be smack in the middle of the circle of danger that surrounded him.

Not good. Not good at all.

Hell.

He'd spent an entire career drawing people in, not pushing them away. He didn't really know how to do it. So maybe, in trying to allay Liza's curiosity by acting like a normal guy, all he'd done was make the situation worse. If he tried to push her away now, she might only get more curious.

Somehow he had to ditch her in a way that would replace her curiosity with something uglier, something that would keep her safely away from him.

Because he was a walking target, no matter how many layers they put around him. There was a big red bull's-eye on his back.

And he didn't want it on Liza's, as well.

Chapter 4

The itch wouldn't quit. Questions answered in a way that didn't reveal a whole lot, a brief hesitation when he said he'd joined the "department,"—those things wouldn't leave Liza alone. What's more, after their nice day on the mountain, he'd avoided her as if she had the plague. That made her mad and convinced her he was hiding something. All that friendly openness, and now he cut her off?

She was fighting a losing battle, certain now that something was wrong with him. And then, a week later, she discovered that he was staying at the La-Z-Rest motel.

For heaven's sake, who stayed there when there were so many apartments available?

There was only one answer: someone who wanted to leave on a minute's notice, and didn't want to have to fill out one of those nosy rental questionnaires.

Except surely the college had been even nosier?

Maybe, but the college protected personnel files a whole lot better than the apartment house protected lessee information. Six days a week she could walk into the rental office and find an opportunity to look in their files. Not so at the college.

Where was he getting his personal mail? At his office? The college didn't like that any more than they liked office computers being used for personal affairs.

So he'd be using a post office box. Very unrevealing. A man with no traceable address.

Then she remembered her conversation with Gage and realized that Gage had deflected her, too. Not that she expected him to spill everything he knew about Max, but the indirect way he had answered when she asked if Max was clean bugged her. "The college hired him, didn't they?" Or words to that effect. Words that had told her nothing at all, and failed to directly answer her question. At the time she'd put it down to Gage not wanting to reveal confidential information. Now she wasn't so sure.

Okay, that did it. Time to break out the big guns. She sat down at her desk and picked up the phone.

"Anything you can find," she told Michele, a friend who still worked for the newspaper, after giving her everything she knew about Max. "Anything."

"Is he that attractive?" Michele asked on a laugh.

That drew Liza up short, but only momentarily. "Yes," she admitted. "But it's not just that. I'm serious about this, Michele."

"I'm sure you are." But Michele was still laughing. "Okay, I've got it, but you know I have to be careful. They're monitoring our use, if you recall."

"I recall. I'm going to keep looking on my end."

"I have no doubt," came the dry response.

Liza hung up, wondering if Michele had hit the nail on the head. Maybe her fear of the attraction she felt was part of this—attraction had never brought much good into her life.

No, she told herself sternly. A guy who lives in a motel and talks about as much as a clam? In her experience when you asked a man about himself, he was only too eager to talk. Usually too much.

Something was definitely not right. And sooner or later she was determined to have some way to beard Max. She couldn't escape the feeling he was hiding something important.

Or hiding from something.

She glanced at her reflection in the window near her elbow. "And aren't you going to feel just wonderful when you find out he's hiding from an ex and alimony?"

Actually, yes. Because if he was that type, she wanted no part of him. News like that would be sure to crush all those damned flutters she felt whenever she saw him.

And since Saturday, she'd hardly seen him at all. Which was another thing. She could have sworn she had seen heat in his gaze a few times. The day had seemed to go well. So why would he be avoiding her? Because she asked too many questions.

But they weren't the crazy-making questions her other boyfriend had complained about. No, these were ordinary getting-to-know-you questions.

This time that excuse wasn't going to cut it.

She nodded her head sharply as if agreeing emphatically with her own reasoning. She'd allowed herself to be dissuaded and distracted for a while, but no more.

And Max would never know anyway. How could he unless she threw it in his face?

Living in a motel? Come on.

Much as it annoyed her to have to spend money on background checks she used to get for free, she ponied up.

She wanted to know everything she could find about Maxwell McKinney, Esquire, J.D., former cop.

Then she hit LexisNexis, the law and news database that the college subscribed to for faculty and student research.

Maxwell McKenny brought up absolutely nothing. Nothing. Okay, he hadn't been involved in any legal cases of note, and had never been in the papers. That would be true of a lot of people.

Search engines also came up blank except for the college site, so he didn't use social networking, didn't have a webpage and had never written anything that was posted online.

At least not this Max McKenny. Almost all the links were for law firms and businesses. And that alone was weird.

Finally one of her cheaper background searches kicked back some info. It listed him as an instructor at the college and gave the college address. No list of past addresses.

She was sitting there drumming her fingers, beginning to think the guy she had talked to didn't exist when the credit check came back: one credit card, three months old, no balance but a credit line of five thousand dollars.

One credit card? Three months old?

She asked for a past history and let out a breath. There was one, although it was sparse. No disputes, no bad ratings, just a slender credit card record for the past eight years.

It showed paid-off student loans—okay, he'd had student loans—and an address in Michigan for the past few years. He must have been renting because the house was owned by some organization that identified itself with a long string of initials…that lead nowhere. Okay, so it wasn't a big apartment company, probably some little guy who had incorporated.

She sighed and leaned back, rolling her shoulders. So he was just an ordinary guy who'd made few waves on the surface of life. And hadn't Gage already told her that when he said, "He got hired, didn't he?"

The only thing left to do was to start calling every police jurisdiction in Michigan and say she was a relative looking for Max McKenny. How far would that get her?

She closed her eyes, considering. It wouldn't be worth the phone bill, she decided. He didn't work there anymore, and that would be the most anyone would tell her, assuming they even admitted they recognized the name.

Cops were a very protective breed.

She hated to admit it, but Max was exactly what he said he was, and living in a motel only made him a tad weird. Sheesh, if she asked him, he'd probably just say he was saving for a house.

So she had just wasted a lot of time because something was niggling at her, mainly the way he seemed to withhold details. Like what department he'd been with.

She sat up a little straighter, considering that. Most cops immediately answered that with the name of the city or state they'd worked for. In her experience, the only time they said "the department" was when there was no question of which department.

She replayed the statement in her mind, and the hesitation seemed to grow larger. His speech wasn't ordinarily hesitant. Far from it.

The man was hiding something.

She wanted to bang her head on the desk. She was going in circles and getting nowhere. Every time she just about had herself convinced that there was no mystery to Max, she would think of something else that didn't seem quite right.

But had she really called Michele to check on the guy? Oh, man. She was losing it. Time to take a break.

She pushed back from the desk and went to get her jogging clothes on. A run would do her a world of good. Maybe even distract her from what was beginning to strike her as a mild form of insanity.

Max was having a bad day. He had avoided Liza since their day out riding, a week ago. Maybe that had been a mistake. The few times he had caught sight of her on campus, she had looked at him with something between hurt and fury. Not that he could blame her. If there were gentle methods for pushing people away, they weren't part of his experience.

He felt like hell about his mishandling of this entire thing. He should have just stayed away completely. God, this situation was giving him nightmares of the kind he hadn't had in a while. He was waking up at night from horrific dreams about the guys who were hunting him, dreams where they got their hands on Liza—and he knew only too well what they were capable of.

He'd lost count of the times he'd awakened with Liza's voice in his head: *Who are you, Max?*

Hell, he couldn't even answer that question for himself anymore.

Oddly, his conscience was troubling him more over his treatment of Liza than over any of the awful, ugly betrayals of trust that made up his entire career.

God, how many times had he lied? He couldn't count them. Couldn't even remember them. His whole damn life was a lie, and now it was tainting someone else whether he wanted it to or not.

He grew hypervigilant again—getting adrenaline rushes over something seen out of the corner of his eye or some unexpected sound, watching ordinary people with distrust and suspicion, people who didn't deserve it.

Just how messed up was he?

Then he got a call on his cell from Ames. "Enders is researching you again, and so is a reporter from St. Petersburg."

"Must be a friend of hers."

"Probably. Damn it, Max, what did you say to her?"

"Nothing."

"Then maybe you better start saying something. With the name change, we weren't expecting anyone to be checking your background, and now someone is. Two someones. I've got guys scrambling to try to plug holes we never thought we'd have to plug."

"What can she find out?"

"Nothing. That's the problem, isn't it? If she were just any other person, you could ignore it. I checked her background. She's a damn good investigative reporter. She's going to hit our walls and get suspicious."

"Apparently she already is suspicious," Max snapped.

"Well, figure out something to tell her. Everything's vague enough that you can fill in the blanks almost any way you want. Hell, you can mostly tell her the truth. Talk about your childhood. Damn it, Max, you do this stuff all the time. You don't need my advice."

Maybe he did. Because this time whatever he was doing wasn't working, and he'd worked with some pretty suspicious people over the years.

Of course, never before had he needed to play an ordinary nice guy.

Hell's bells!

The Harley found its own way over to Liza's apartment. Just as he parked, she came out the front door and started stretching like she was going to run. Then she spied him and froze.

"Hi," he called, slinging his helmet over the handlebars and approaching her.

"Hi," she said cautiously.

"Going for a run?"

"That was the plan."

"Mind if I ride alongside you? I'm not dressed for running."

She stared daggers at him. "Get lost."

"I need to talk to you. Let me just tag along."

She hesitated for an eternity, and part of him hoped she would tell him to go to hell. Then he could shovel this all back to Ames and keep clear of this woman. She disappointed him.

"If you keep your exhaust out of my face."

So he putted alongside her, occasionally using his feet for balance at the slow speed. "Sorry I haven't been around," he said by way of opening. "I got busy. You were right about all those girls."

She laughed brittlely at that, but just kept pounding the sidewalk.

"They come up with some amazing questions," he volunteered.

"They want your attention."

"They're even more inquisitive than you are."

At that she gave him a sidelong glance. "Really."

"Really." It was a gorgeous autumn day, with leaves starting to turn everywhere, the sun warm on his skin, the air cool. But compared to seeing Liza run, nature didn't even take second place. He supposed she was wearing one of those sports bras, but it didn't take the fun out of watching the bounce of her breasts. He had to remind himself to pay attention to the street ahead. Remind himself that he was pure poison and shouldn't even entertain these thoughts.

"So," he said, struck by a moment of inspiration, "my credit reporting service said you checked my credit."

That froze her so suddenly that she almost stumbled. He braked and shot out an arm to catch her elbow, steadying her.

"Oh," she said.

He almost laughed. Might have laughed if he weren't so annoyed by all this. "Didn't expect that?" he asked, and couldn't quite keep the irritation from his voice.

"Uh, no," she admitted honestly. Then she turned to face him, putting her hands on her hips. "You want to yell at me?"

"No, I want to know what's driving you crazy."

She scowled. "I keep telling myself I'm in hyperdrive, that I shouldn't give a darn who you are, but for some reason something about you isn't right."

He'd never heard that before, not from anyone but her. Damn, he was losing his touch. "Like what?"

"Like you living in that run-down motel. This town is full of empty, cheap apartments. Nobody would choose to actually live at the La-Z-Rest."

"Maybe I'm not sure yet that I'll want to keep on teaching."

"Maybe?" Her frown deepened and she pointed a finger at him. "The last time I met someone as evasive as you, it was a politician who was dipping his fingers in the public till. I keep telling myself that you're just closemouthed, and maybe that's a cop thing, but you know what? My nose doesn't believe it."

She had a good nose, he thought. "I smell like rotten fish?"

He was glad to see her frown crack a bit. "Sort of," she answered.

His sigh was real. "Maybe we should talk. How badly do you want to run?"

"Very badly. It's better than beating my head on a brick wall."

Ames's words came back to him. She'd definitely noticed. "We can meet at Maude's and I'll buy you lunch. Say in an hour?"

She tilted her head, studying him with those cat-green eyes as if she might see into him. Or through him. Edginess began to make the back of his neck prickle, a sure warning sign.

Then she stepped forward. "Give me that extra helmet. Let's make it brunch, and right now."

He hoped like hell that she didn't guess how much he liked having her ride pillion, all wrapped around him.

In fact, he took some corners a little too fast just so she would hold on tighter.

And he stared grimly down the streets, wondering what pack of lies he was going to invent this time. God, he so wanted to be done with this.

As they drove, he kept scanning for the least little thing that seemed out of place. He couldn't afford to relax. Not now. Not ever, maybe. That target was still on his back.

Maude's was having a midmorning lull. A group of aging ranchers were enjoying some pie and coffee in the corner, most likely taking a break from a long, hard week before they went to the feed store.

Maude slapped down the menus with the panache that Max was beginning to realize was her usual manner, and poured them both coffee without asking.

"Omelet's good this morning," she said shortly. "Fresh eggs."

Max had already figured out that disagreeing with Maude's menu suggestion could lead to a discussion he didn't feel like having this morning, even though he really didn't want that much to eat. "Omelet it is," he said, smiling.

"Me, too, Maude. Thanks."

Maude stomped away without speaking.

"I wonder what's in the omelet?" Max asked.

"We'll find out," Liza answered, her smile tight.

Okay, time to deal with this crap. Somehow. Oddly, for the first time in years, glib lies didn't spring to his tongue. It frustrated him. What a time to turn honest.

"Honestly," he said, "I feel like I'm drifting and waiting. I'm unsettled. Not sure where I'm going or how to get there."

She nodded encouragingly but surprised him by not

asking a question. It was not what he expected from her and wondered if he had already lost her completely. Then he wondered why it should matter. But it sure as hell did.

Maude returned with fluffy omelets. She slammed the plates down so hard Max was sure his omelet deflated before his eyes. He could see mushrooms and green pepper and bits of ham peeking out at him.

Liza remained silent.

Not good.

With Maude's basilisk eyes on him, he took a mouthful of the omelet and nodded approvingly. Only then did she walk away.

"Why are you so angry with me?" he asked, going on the attack. "Because I'm living in a motel? What's wrong with that, especially when I'm not sure I want to get into a lease?"

"A rolling stone gathers no moss," she quoted, then let it hang.

"So maybe I'm a rolling stone."

"Evidently." She picked up her fork and cut into the omelet.

"Maybe you should tell me what has you so concerned. I feel like I'm caught up in a Kafka novel. I don't know what the questions are, and I seem to be giving all the wrong answers."

Some of the tension seeped out of her. At last she looked at him, and her cat-green eyes were kinder, although not totally devoid of suspicion.

"Maybe I should apologize," she said quietly. "I felt as if you were deflecting me when I asked simple questions, the kind of questions you ask of anyone you just met."

He had been deflecting. He did it as naturally as breathing. "And?"

"And I'm a reporter. When people don't answer questions, I start to wonder what they're hiding. So maybe I went over the top."

"And now that I'm willing to answer questions, you don't have any?"

She shook her head. "What's the point? You're a rolling stone. You said so yourself. So what else do I need to know?"

That knocked him back on his heels. She was writing him off? That easily? After driving him and Ames nuts with all her questions? Although he should be grateful for that, he definitely didn't feel it. Mess, some corner of his mind warned sharply. But he just kept walking into the quicksand.

Now things smelled fishy to him. "What are you doing? Swearing off curiosity?"

She shrugged, and he was surprised to see that she looked a little pained. "As I mentioned, I've been told often that I'm too curious for my own good."

He couldn't deny it. Having her stumble around in his background was raising flags, and one of those flags might come to the attention of the wrong people. After all, the people he was here to get away from had probably figured out who he really worked for as result of the arrests, even if they hadn't found his new identity. They probably had someone hunting for him even harder than Liza. But if they sniffed him out and found her, she could be in trouble. Serious trouble, if she got in their way.

Maybe he should just pack up and go now. The agency could send someone else to cover his teaching position for the semester. Yeah, he should probably just hit the road while he still could.

Yet he remained rooted, because who would watch out for Liza? Nobody but the sheriff knew what Max had on his tail, and while Dalton seemed like a good and capable man, he didn't have the resources to put an indefinite watch on one woman.

He tried to reassure himself that her few queries about him wouldn't get her into trouble. It was him they wanted. But part of him, an instinct he never ignored, was making him uneasy anyway.

She sat there quietly across from him, eating slowly, asking nothing. It was killing him. He knew he should be relieved that she'd given up. She would poke no further into dangerous things. But Liza without questions wasn't really Liza.

"So what do you want to know?" he asked, hoping to get her rolling again.

"Nothing really. It doesn't matter."

He didn't believe it. He didn't want to believe that Liza could be defeated so easily. This woman had raised enough flags to make Ames yell at him, but she was going to give up now?

Just a short time ago she had confronted him about living at the motel. What had happened? His saying he was a rolling stone?

But maybe she didn't believe that, either. Why would she? He'd told her he'd been a cop for eight years. She knew he had finished college and law school. That didn't sound like a résumé for a rolling stone. So maybe she just figured he was lying again.

Which he was. He shifted uncertainly. He hadn't meant that he was always a rolling stone, just that he might not be here permanently.

Had she misunderstood?

Or was she writing him off because she was attracted to him and could see no future in it? He had read her attraction clearly enough; it had been there in the way she looked at him sometimes.

Something else he'd learned to recognize, evaluate and avoid if necessary.

Crap. His life, and he himself, were one big freaking mess now.

And he felt about two inches tall. Somehow he seemed to have crushed this woman. He swallowed another mouthful of omelet, not even tasting it, wondering why something so light should feel like lead in his stomach.

He should just let it lie. Ames would be thrilled if she never wanted to know another thing about him. That was the point, wasn't it? Yet his own feelings said something quite different.

And since when did he have feelings that conflicted with his job?

Since Liza.

He put his fork down and regarded her rather grimly. He had to undo whatever it was he had done to shut her down, yet do so without making her more inquisitive.

People often told her she was too curious? Well, she couldn't be referring to her job. Reporters needed to be curious, to want every question answered.

Then a little light went on. "Who said you were too curious?"

She seemed to fold inward a bit, then finally looked at him. "Boyfriends. One in particular."

"Oh." Well, that might explain it.

"I'm sorry," she said. "It was wrong of me to check your credit history."

"I thought that was the new thing in dating. Background checks."

"We're not dating—you're just a colleague. I guess I just wanted to build a mystery."

No, he thought, she'd homed in with unerring instinct on the fact that he wasn't exactly who he said he was. Now she seemed to be feeling really bad about it, whether because she felt she'd done something wrong, or because she felt her instincts were wrong.

Neither thought made him happy.

He caught Maude glaring his way and picked up his fork again to eat more omelet. She stomped over just long enough to refresh their mugs of coffee, then disappeared back into the kitchen.

"My dad," he said slowly, "was an airline pilot. Mom taught fifth grade."

Liza looked at him again, attentive but saying nothing.

"I grew up wanting to be a pilot," he added. "While I was away at college, they had a break-in and my mom was hurt. Badly. You could say that changed my course."

She nodded. "Did they catch the perp?"

"Yes. And that made my mom feel a little safer— I mean, she'd gone six months by that time, almost afraid of her own shadow. She wouldn't answer the door. Every time someone knocked she jumped a foot. Dad got her a watchdog, and even broke his rule and got her a pistol. It didn't help until they locked up the two guys who had beaten her."

"Two of them? My God!"

"Yeah. Two of them. While my dad was out of town for three days. Anyway, they got the guys who did it, but Mom still didn't feel all that safe so they moved to a place that would have no memories for her." He didn't add that his mom had been held at gunpoint for several terrifying hours, or that the guys who had done it had been members of a militia with a religious overtone and that the whole break-in had been about getting guns that couldn't be traced to them, guns his parents didn't even own. Fringe fanatics hell-bent on facing Armageddon well armed.

"I'm really sorry. So you decided to go into law enforcement instead?"

"I didn't want anybody to feel the way my mother felt. Ever."

Her face softened. She was emerging from wherever she had locked herself up. He wasn't certain that was a good thing, but it was better than the way she'd been acting a few minutes ago.

"But now you've left?" she asked.

No, he hadn't. But he couldn't say that, could he, so the lies had to begin.

"At least for now."

"Burn out?"

"Not exactly." How to explain that? Damn, had he gotten so rusty that he couldn't talk to anyone who wasn't a bad guy? "I just needed some time to think. Most of what a cop does, well, it doesn't save anybody, does it?"

"Sometimes it does seem like too little too late."

"Exactly." And he should leave it right there. Unless she asked another question.

"You wanted to be Superman?"

That question took him by surprise and elicited a laugh. "No such thing." He hesitated, then offered her another small piece of the truth. "I wanted to find a way to prevent bad things. But almost everything in law comes after the fact. After the crime." Almost but not quite, and that was a distinction he couldn't elaborate on.

She surprised him by nodding. "I can imagine. As a reporter I hated it. Sometimes I was lucky enough to tumble onto something that had just started, some malfeasance or other, and stopped it by reporting it, but most of the time, by the time I found out, it was a mess. I hated that about the cop beat. It didn't improve much with government."

He agreed. "But justice must wait on a crime being committed."

"Sad but true." She started eating again, and looked more relaxed. "I'm sorry, Max. Truly. I shouldn't have gone barging into your background."

"Don't apologize. I guess I spent too many years asking the questions and not answering them." Good at deflecting and lying. Now wouldn't that look great on a résumé?

"So where do your parents live now?"

"In Ireland."

"For real? Why Ireland?"

"My mom has roots there. They have a little cottage in a little town where they know everyone, and Mom feels safe there."

"That's a long move to find safety."

He nodded. Just then Maude advanced on them again.

"Omelets okay?"

"They're great," he and Liza answered almost in unison.

Then she put down two cheesy hash-brown casseroles and walked away.

Max eyed them. "I don't think we ordered those."

"No." A little giggle escaped Liza. "Maude likes to take care of people."

"Put them in the cardiac unit, you mean."

"Eat up. You can come run it off with me later."

"What about you?" he asked, one of his leading deflection questions. "You grew up here?"

"I did. Both my parents taught school."

"And now?"

"You're not going to believe me."

He liked the sudden sparkle in her eyes. "No? Try me."

"My dad had the nickname Noah. Do you see any water around here?"

"Other than creeks and streams, no."

"Exactly. But one day when I was about ten, he decided he wanted a boat. A nice one. And he wanted to sail around the world. Well, you can't afford a boat on a teacher's salary, so he started building one."

"Wow!" He smiled as he envisioned it. "That's amazing."

"It was. At first it caused a lot of jokes. I mean, who builds a forty-foot boat in their backyard in a place as dry as this? But he did. Piece by piece as he could afford it and as the weather allowed. After a while, neighbors started to help out. Anyway, five years ago she was launched in a reservoir up north of here. She proved seaworthy, so not too long after that, they were off. First they sailed the East and West Coasts, and now they're going around the world. The last I heard, they'd made it across the Pacific and were in Australia."

"That's awesome! Do you ever want to join them?"

"Sometimes. But they're having so much fun I sort of feel like I'd be intruding. It's just the two of them, something they didn't have for most of their lives. I just keep telling them to avoid the Indian Ocean."

"Do you think they will?"

"Yeah, my dad's no fool and he'd never be reckless with my mother. I suspect around the world will leave out a chunk."

"Good. I'd have kittens if I thought my folks might sail anywhere near those pirates."

"There are pirates everywhere from what my dad says. They're just cautious. And armed."

"Very little law out there on the high seas," he remarked.

She nodded.

"Still, I can see the draw in it. It sounds wonderful, to be out there away from everything. And think of all the places you could visit."

"I know. They've emailed me tons of pictures. Sometimes I just look at them and dream."

So the inquisitor had dreams? That touched him. He wasn't sure he had any left himself, beyond finishing this current mess. After that…who knew?

They finished their lunch companionably enough, talking about their classes. But after he paid, she left him on the street to continue her jog. Her back announced it was done between them.

Mission accomplished. He guessed it was her observation that he was a rolling stone. He should be relieved, but he wasn't.

He watched her go, admiring her figure and wishing he was just an ordinary teacher, one who could ask her for a date and eventually make love to her.

He couldn't remember the last time a woman made him feel so hot and bothered. Nor could he remember one he had less right to approach.

When she disappeared around a corner, he sighed and climbed back onto his bike.

Some things weren't meant to be, and this one had been killed at the very first lie: his name.

Live with it. It was all part of the job. He sure as hell ought to know that by now.

Well, he did know it. But this time he hated it. An unfamiliar anger filled him, as he thought about all the things, ordinary things, he'd had to skip over and do without because of his damn job.

Then he felt like a fool. He'd volunteered for this. Nobody had held him at gunpoint. So what if now he was feeling like he'd made a heap of bad decisions?

He rode slowly around town, becoming more familiar with his surroundings, alert for anything that didn't look quite right. His life depended on knowing the usual from the unusual. He'd memorized the campus, but he still had some work to do on the town.

And how the hell had he ever thought he'd be able to shuck it all for a while by coming to the back of nowhere?

Because he had wished it. As simple as that. It was what he had wanted.

Too bad he wasn't getting it. Every single one of his demons had dogged his steps.

The group in the ruined building sat around on mattresses, smoking and waiting. Jody had so far been unable to break through the firewall with ATF, even with the agent's real name. Two days wasted, and the message that had made its way out from federal detention said their leaders were getting impatient. They'd been in the can for nearly four months now, and they were starting to make threats.

Rose stood up and reached for one of the two inexpensive dresses she'd bought at a secondhand store, both of which made her look cheap and easy. She ground a cigarette butt under her unlaced boot, then shook both her boots off. She pulled the blue dress off the wire hanger, tugged it over her head, shucked her fatigues and then tugged the spandex dress all the way on. She didn't care about the eyes on her. They didn't dare touch her.

"I'll get more out of the guy tonight," she said with assurance. She pulled the clasp out of her hair and ran a brush through it, then sprayed some cheap perfume in the air around her. Moments later, she tapped out the door in spiky heels, wrapped once again in the olive drab jacket.

"She probably will," Jody remarked as he listened to her disappear out the back way. "All I need is one more clue."

Nobody argued with him.

"We're gonna fry Max," agreed one of the others.

"Not until Rose uses her knife," another said.

They all laughed.

Chapter 5

After her shower, Liza settled in to grade her students' first news stories. She knew from experience that the lede was going to give them the most trouble. That first sentence was always the biggest headache.

She had given them a list of facts about an accident and guidelines for writing, and they'd spent the first week of classes talking about ledes, how they were important, what they had to do. They were the absolute focus of the story in one short sentence.

They'd probably be at least halfway through the semester before she started to get any acceptable ledes at all.

Many experienced working reporters still had problems with ledes, and every reporter needed to have a lede rewritten from time to time.

At least her students had enjoyed her explanation for why papers had started spelling *lead* as *lede*. Back in the old days of typesetting, *lead* had referred to the type. So to distinguish in their markups, newspapers had started misspelling the word so the typesetters wouldn't misunderstand.

It was one of those bits of arcana that always tickled students to learn. Jargon. Made them feel like insiders.

But it sure didn't help them write the dang things.

Four hours later she had a bit of a headache from reading her students' attempts. Each one had to be re-written, not just criticized, in order for the student to learn.

Even on her busiest day on the job she'd only had to write four ledes. This afternoon she had gone through more than forty. Ugh. Not even an editor needed to repair or even read that many.

Rubbing her stiff neck, she went to close the window she had opened a few inches. The late afternoon was growing chilly as the sun sank behind mountains, and while it wouldn't get dark yet for a while, the air cooled off quickly.

Just as she closed the window, she heard the chime that announced new email. Hoping for a note from her parents, she hurried back to her computer.

Instead she found an email from Michele.

Don't know where you got that this guy graduated from Stetson Law. Was it from the college? Our morgue lists all the graduates each year, and he's not on the list. The closest I could come to the name you gave me was Kenneth Maxwell. Sorry.

Liza felt as if she had just been doused with cold water. She sat frozen in shock as if everything inside her had jumbled up. Her muscles weakened.

Just as she had started to think this guy was above-board, this came in? Just as she had started to think he was finally being open with her?

She could hardly catch her breath. This couldn't be right. The damn college had him listed as a Stetson grad.

As soon as she could move again, she sent Michele a hasty email: R U sure?

Three minutes later the response came back:

I checked the last ten years, all Stetson J.D.s awarded. You know we list the grads.

Yes, they did. Just as they did for all the local high schools and colleges. Each year, all the area schools who wanted to be included sent the lists of names, and the paper printed exactly what it received.

The difference between Maxwell McKenny and Kenneth Maxwell was too huge to be a typo and too similar to be a coincidence.

Anger came to her rescue, flooding her. She checked the Stetson list of grads again, and there he was. But he wasn't on the paper's list. And the paper wouldn't have made a mistake of that magnitude. No way.

She sat biting her lip, drumming her fingers. Telling herself to just drop it, it was none of her business, and knowing damn well she wasn't going to drop it if only because she hated being lied to. Absolutely hated it.

She went to the newspaper's archives, punching in her credit card number, not caring what it cost. And what she found made her feel even colder: the list of graduates from the year Max had graduated was not available. It had been removed from the archives.

She hesitated, then picked up the phone. "Michele?

Sorry to bother you, but I just checked the paper's archives and there's no list of graduates for the year this guy got his J.D."

Michele was silent for a moment. "That's not possible. I saw it yesterday. Let me check again."

Liza waited while keys tapped in the background. Maybe because Michele was still working there she could get at files that Liza couldn't. Maybe.

"It's gone," Michele said after a full minute. "I don't understand it. I saw it yesterday, Liza, I swear. All the years were here."

"Thanks, Michele."

"You want me to burrow more? Now I'm curious."

Liza was tempted but didn't want to get Michele into any trouble. "No, no. Thanks. The paper will rag on you if you're not working on a story. It's okay. I can keep checking from here."

"You're sure? What's going on with this guy, anyway? Did he do something?"

"He didn't do anything," Liza said. "Not anything."

"Except get your attention."

"Yeah. Except that. It doesn't really matter."

"He must be one hell of a dish," Michele replied, trying to lighten things.

"Not anymore he isn't."

No, he was a rotten liar. Come to that, he was a lousy liar. He'd almost had her convinced he was just what he seemed, even though he'd figured out she'd done a background on him. Why hadn't he just come clean?

And who the hell could erase newspaper archives?

Madder than a wasp, she started searching online for any news in Michigan and Florida about Kenneth Maxwell: Kenneth Maxwell, J.D.; Kenneth Maxwell,

Esquire; Ken Maxwell…every formulation she could think of.

While she went through law databases and news articles, she felt at once frightened of what she might find and exhilarated as if she were a bloodhound on a trail.

It seemed to take forever. The night darkened until she had to switch on a light. The numbers of papers and databases she searched was huge, and her credit card was starting to get antsy. She didn't care. She wanted the truth.

And when at last it hit her, she sat in even deeper shock. A little blurb from her old newspaper, listing the more interesting jobs that the Stetson grads were getting: Prosecutor's Office, Public Defender's Office, this or that law firm…and Kenneth Maxwell, ATF.

He'd gone to the Bureau of Alcohol, Tobacco and Firearms?

Almost instinctively, as if her computer might explode, she shut down her browser and turned it off. ATF.

No wonder he wasn't telling her the truth.

But now she had a million more questions. Questions she couldn't ask. Even reporters knew they couldn't interfere in an ongoing investigation. What the hell was going on in Conard County?

And somehow she wasn't at all surprised when her doorbell rang a half hour later.

Max stood there looking like wrath personified. His blue eyes blazed with fire rather than ice. His leather jacket hung open, and his dark hair was tousled as if he'd ridden over to her place without a helmet. He jabbed a finger at her. "You're in trouble."

"I didn't do anything."

"You did plenty." He didn't wait for an invitation,

simply brushed past her into her apartment and closed the door. "Anyone else here?"

She almost lied and said someone was in her bedroom, because right now he frightened her. But then her spine stiffened.

"No."

"Good." He glared at her. "Sit down."

"No."

He blew out a loud breath of frustration, and put his hands on his narrow hips. "You couldn't let it go, could you. I thought you'd stopped."

"I had."

"But? What do you call what you've been doing for the past four hours? You've got flags popping all over the country now. I got a call to shut you down now. Before they decide to pick you up."

"I haven't done anything wrong!" Her anger flared, partly from fear. Picked up? For what? "Not one damn thing."

"No? You just may have walked yourself into a pack of trouble, Liza. A real giant-size pack of federal trouble."

"I didn't do anything," she repeated stubbornly. "Why should flags be popping anywhere?"

"Because if you could put two and two together, so can someone else. And that someone might find that all of that stuff you were digging around in leads back here. You're messing in a federal investigation."

She tried to keep glaring at him, but as his words penetrated, she felt her muscles growing watery. She had no idea what was going on, but words like *obstruction of justice* started popping into her head.

She was no coward. More than once someone had threatened her life and she'd just kept investigating.

But this was somehow different. An ATF agent was accusing her of messing up a federal investigation. The penalties for that were much more real and much more frightening than some sheriff shooting off his mouth. It unnerved her.

Slowly she sank onto her secondhand couch. "Max... Ken..."

"Max. Everyone calls me Max. Saves trouble."

She stole a look upward at him. "Believe it or not, I can keep my mouth shut, but you've got to tell me what I'm doing wrong. How can my finding out who you are put an investigation in danger?"

He ran his fingers impatiently through his shaggy hair, then pulled her desk chair over and straddled it, facing her. His expression was grim.

"I unrolled an operation a couple of months ago. We didn't manage to round up everyone, and I'm the key witness. So they'd very much like to see me dead."

"Oh." Things started clicking in her brain, coming together with a general outline. "You were undercover."

"Very."

"Why aren't you in a safe house?"

"Because I'd go crazy. Because everyone, me included, thought my own personal, temporary form of the witness protection plan would work. Nobody counted on you."

"Oh," she said again, and couldn't help but feel a flicker of pride. "But nobody else knows your name. Certainly not the bad guys?"

"They don't. Yet. We think. But you do. And if you could figure it all out..." He didn't complete the thought. "You've got my handler jumping like a cat on a hot stove. He's absolutely furious, mostly at me because I couldn't deflect you."

"I knew you were deflecting me," she said irritably. "It seemed obvious to me."

"No kidding. I'm usually better than this."

"And they didn't do a very good job of hiding you."

He snorted. "Nobody was expecting inquiries from this end. Nobody expected someone who knew my current alias to be looking into my background. You've had them jumping around trying to patch holes, change databases…" He paused, and the faintest of smiles touched his hard mouth. "You're very good, Liza. You've had us in overdrive."

That gave her some satisfaction, but she had to admit it was less than she ordinarily would have felt. Mainly because she might have endangered Max.

"What was the tip-off?" he asked. "We need to know."

"A reporter friend couldn't find you in the news archives as a graduate from the law school. But she found a similar name. The thing is, when I went to look myself, that particular story had vanished. You left a hole."

He nodded. "So the hole grabbed you?"

"Well, I certainly wondered who would have the power to alter a newspaper's archives. So I went searching."

"We noticed," he said drily.

"And came up with a blurb about Kenneth Maxwell joining the ATF."

He sighed, clenching and unclenching his fingers as if to release tension.

"But the bad guys don't know your real name. And I promise I won't tell anyone."

"I'm sure you won't. The thing is, Liza, the more we go around changing databases and trying to separate me from my former alias, the easier it gets to do something noticeable. Like the change to the newspaper archives. One slip, and I'm out."

"But they can protect you."

"But what about you?" he countered, stunning her. "You've done enough searches to link yourself to my current alias and my real name. If these guys find out either one, they'll be looking at you. You certainly put a spotlight on yourself."

"There's no reason to think anyone else will make the connections."

"Really?" He rubbed his chin. "I know for a fact these guys have a great hacker working for them. We've got these guys on conspiracy to commit acts of terror, illegal arms possession, possession of explosives, bomb-building…a whole impressive array of crimes. They're dangerous, they're fanatics and they'd step on you like a bug if they thought you were involved because they don't care who they kill, and they sure as hell don't want to spend life in prison."

Cold began to seep through her. Not the cold she had felt when she realized he had lied about his name. No, this was something different, something even more disturbing. She'd been a reporter long enough to know what violence was. She knew it intimately and had seen its results.

She rubbed her palms on her jeans, realizing they had dampened with fear. She tried to remember the last time she had felt this afraid and couldn't. Not even when that corrupt sheriff had reminded her there were lots of isolated places in his county and people disappeared all the time. Not even then.

This was different. This time she might face a group

of people who weren't making stupid threats, people who would actually carry them out.

But no way was she going to apologize. "If you'd just told me the truth, I would have left it alone." She lifted her gaze and found his angry blue eyes had quieted some. If anything, they looked troubled.

"How often," he asked after a moment or two, "do you think someone in my position thinks it would be wise to break cover?"

"Not often," she admitted.

"Exactly. So tell me why in the world I would look at you, at a few passing questions and think that I should just spill it all?"

Most people, even former reporters, would probably have blown it off. But not her. She'd always been unwilling to let anything go that awoke her curiosity. "My boyfriend was right," she admitted grimly. "I ask too many questions."

He didn't answer immediately. She peeked at him again and found him looking worried.

"I guess," he said finally, "that I put up too many warning flags myself. They might have worked with someone else, but I should have made a more careful effort. I didn't do my job right."

She didn't have any idea how to respond to that, so she just waited.

"My boss was right," he continued a minute later. "He said I'd screwed up, that I could do better."

"So why did you screw up?"

"Maybe because I'm sick of living a constant lie."

"But that's your job."

"It doesn't make it any more palatable. Yeah, I'm trying to prevent bad things from happening. I devoted eight years of my life to exactly that. Eight years of pretending to be what I'm not. Of never letting anyone get too close. Eight years of lies and deflections. Maybe I was just getting tired of it. I am tired of it."

She felt a strong wave of sympathy for him. "I can't imagine it."

He shrugged. "Sometimes I wonder if I know who I really am anymore. I've been pretending for too long. So maybe I slipped up on purpose. Maybe at some level I just wanted to quit lying. It's a lousy excuse, though, and it could have endangered the investigation, and there's a remote chance it could endanger you."

"We don't know that for sure." In fact, it was all too easy to convince herself that the links he feared would never be made. He was probably just being overly cautious, right? She was a nobody teacher in a town he'd just come to. The real danger was to him and his investigation.

"No, we don't know for sure. But the bottom line is now we have to be on guard. Not just for me, but for you, as well. And that's my fault."

"I don't think you should blame yourself. I knew the instant I saw you that something wasn't right. That's why I came over. I was sure there was an interesting story."

He offered her a humorless half smile. "More than you bargained for."

"No reporter ever bargains for a dull story."

He gave a little shake of his head, but fell silent. Then he said, "I think I'm done with lies."

"So how much was a lie?"

"Too little. That's how you sensed things weren't right." He stood and started pacing her small living room, seeming to fill every inch of it. "Okay. No more lies. My name is indeed Kenneth Maxwell. McKenny was my mother's maiden name. Everyone calls me Max, like I said, except my folks. To them I'm Ken or Kenny. I did grow up in Michigan. I got my law degree in the break between two undercover jobs. The first one was in Miami. The last one in Michigan. The Miami job involved gun smuggling. This last one was about domestic terrorism. And it was the job I most wanted because of what happened to my mother."

Her heart squeezed. She could almost feel his pain. "I can understand that."

"It took me years to get on the inside of the Michigan group, Liza. Years. I spent an awful lot of time on the fringe before they trusted me enough to take me inside. Once I had enough evidence, a team arrived to roll them up, but a few of them managed to get away."

"And they're the ones you're hiding from."

"Yes. We got all the major players. The rest though…" He shrugged. "They're fanatics. True believers. They'll do anything they're told to do, and anything they think necessary to get their leaders out of prison. Anything to stop the trial."

"And you have to hide from them until the trial?"

"At least. Or until we get them."

"How many are missing?"

"Six. It's enough. If they can silence me, the case will start to fall apart. That's got to be their primary goal right now."

"How long before the trial?"

"Months. A long time. If you know anything about federal prosecutors, you know they don't move without dotting every *i* and crossing every *t*. They want an ironclad case."

"That's a long time to hang in limbo." Instinctively she glanced toward the windows and wondered if she should draw the curtains. But that was ridiculous. Nobody out there would care that Max was pacing in her living room. At least not yet. Even if she had planted Day-Glo signs pointing toward him from Michigan, they couldn't have arrived already. And so far, they didn't even know if her poking around had gotten back to the fanatics.

But she still felt uneasy, and a bit of a fool. She really had had no reason to check into Max the way she had. She wasn't on a story; she had no proof that he'd done something wrong.

"I was selfish," she announced.

He stopped pacing to look at her. "Selfish?"

"Yes. I wanted to satisfy my curiosity. Use my skills. Feel the rush of being on a story again. It's true I felt you were hiding something, but whatever it was, it wasn't my business. Not at all. I'm sorry."

"You did what comes naturally. No need to apologize. And I should have had my guard up. Too late now."

He sat again, this time on the couch near her. "Maybe I should apologize to you."

"Me?"

"For lying. For not deflecting you well enough. For dragging you into this mess, however unintentionally." He shook his head again. "Damn it, Ames is right. I'm better than this. I slipped up big-time."

She thought about that, trying to decide how she felt about what he was saying. There was only one thing she knew for sure. "I hate being lied to. So I guess I'm glad that part is over."

He arched a brow at her. "I'm forgiven?"

"It feels weird to forgive you for doing your job. I mean, the instant I saw your name associated with ATF,

I felt awful. I completely understood why you weren't answering my questions. I'm just glad to know I didn't blow your cover on an operation here."

"No, I'm just trying to keep a low profile."

In spite of herself, she laughed. "I guess that didn't work so well."

"Not well enough."

Then he surprised her by sliding closer, until their hips touched. "I haven't killed the magic?"

All of a sudden, breathing was difficult. "Magic?"

"This," he said, and kissed her.

For an instant, astonishment gripped her. This was no first kiss, tentative and leaving her wondering how she would accept it. No, this was a full, deep and demanding kiss. He wrapped his arms tightly around her, and plunged his tongue into her as if he owned her.

For one dizzying moment she wanted to object to his presumption. She was an independent woman who made her own decisions about things like this. But for over a week now she'd been thinking of him, longing for him, having totally uncharacteristic urges to be taken like a cavewoman. Even her hard-learned distrust of men hadn't been enough to kill her hunger for him.

Desire swamped her in heat. The attraction she'd been feeling from the start grew into a conflagration. She melted like steel in a superheated fire. Even her bones seemed to turn liquid.

She answered the thrust of his tongue eagerly and lifted her arms to hold him as tightly as he held her.

It felt so good. It had been so long since she had been held like this, with passion and need. As if he was almost desperate for the connection.

And he had called it magic. A good name for the alchemy happening inside her as her body awoke to a deep-rooted ache of longing. She tried to get even closer as his tongue plundered her mouth, teaching her that a mere kiss could lift her to the summit.

But this was no mere kiss. It felt as if he dived into her entire body in a rhythm every cell recognized and responded to.

He lifted his head briefly; she gasped air into her lungs. Murmuring something she couldn't understand, he shifted her, and the next thing she knew she was lying on her back on the couch and he was lying on top of her.

She had forgotten how good a man's weight could feel. Just the pressure, the sense of his angles and planes meeting her softer curves. The way he covered her, at once sheltering and claiming.

His mouth found hers again, sweeping her away on another kiss. But now he could move his hands and he did so, first cradling her head for his assault on her mouth, then trailing one down slowly, filling her with breathless anticipation as he caressed her neck. Shivers of delight ran through her, and impatience began to build. She wanted ever so much more.

Lower his hand slipped until it cupped her breast. Not even layers of clothing could stop the shock of excitement that exploded in her as he kneaded her gently. Helplessly, she arched against him with a soft moan and her legs separated, inviting him closer.

Now she could feel his hardness against her most sensitive place. The ache built, causing her to lift again toward him, seeking satisfaction.

He broke their kiss and nibbled at her ear, causing more delight to shiver through her. His tongue found the side of her throat, teasing her to even greater heights of sensitivity.

And all the while, her hips fell into a rhythm that he soon joined. The ache between her legs grew so intense it almost hurt as he rubbed himself against her in the most exciting way imaginable.

She had never made love fully clothed before. Hadn't even considered it. But she knew where she was going now, and the barriers of denim and leather made it somehow even more exciting.

She struggled to lift her legs, to open herself even more, to wrap him in them, but before she could do that, before she was even ready for what was about to happen, she exploded in an orgasm so intense it dragged a deep moan from her. An instant later he gasped, and while pinwheels still whirled behind her eyelids, she felt him go heavy and limp. And then he settled in more firmly, cradling her tightly with his arms.

Sense returned slowly. Reluctantly. His mouth was near her ear, and she could feel the warmth of his breath tickling her as aftershocks rippled through her.

"Are you okay?" he whispered.

"Oh, yeah," she managed to say. She felt him drop a kiss on her earlobe, and responded by tightening her arms around him.

"I'm not usually such a caveman," he murmured.

The words so closely paralleled some of her own thoughts that a small laugh escaped her. "I'm not complaining."

"Maybe now I'll be able to think again."

She could have taken the words wrong, but she didn't. She wondered if either of them had been thinking very clearly since the first instant of attraction. Maybe not.

She lifted a languid hand, surprised by how weak she felt, and ran her fingertips through his hair. "What's so important about thinking?"

"Nothing, at the moment." Humor laced his tone.

"Good." She didn't want to move. She didn't want him to move. She wanted these minutes to last forever.

But nothing lasts forever. Finally he sighed and rolled off her, coming to kneel by the couch and look into her eyes. "You're sure you're okay?"

"Never better."

She liked the way his icy blue eyes could warm up as they did now. She loved his smile. "I guess you can tell your boss that you've successfully called off the dogs."

"I hope not because of this."

She gave a little shake of her head and reluctantly let him help her sit up. Every inch of her felt drained and relaxed. Her head fell back against the couch and she closed her eyes.

She felt him sit beside her, then he took her hand, squeezing gently and holding it. She squeezed back, liking the dry warmth of his skin. What next, she wondered. Would he stay or go? Should she offer him something to drink or eat?

It appalled her to realize that she didn't know what step to take next. Most likely because the relationship between them, such as it was, hadn't followed a normal pattern. When added to the fact that dating had been mostly an irregularity in her life, she didn't have a whole lot of experience to guide her.

She turned her head a little and opened her eyes to see that he was sitting much as she was, head back, eyes closed. Legs stretched out loosely in front of him.

Oh, boy, he hadn't even taken off his leather jacket. For some reason that made a blush start to warm her cheeks. She'd heard of teens behaving this way, but adults?

She snapped her eyes closed, suddenly afraid to make eye contact. Suddenly worried about what he might think of her. The word *easy* sprang to mind, and she didn't at all like the thought of wearing it.

Then she scolded herself. She was a modern woman. Where were these feelings coming from? Some ancient cavern of the past, obviously, one she didn't even consider part of her life.

"Liza?"

"Hmm." She kept her eyes closed.

"Are you all right?"

"Why do you ask?"

"Your breathing changed."

Great. He could read her like an open book. But what did she expect from an ATF agent who worked undercover?

At least that's who he said he was.

All of a sudden her eyes snapped open and she turned to look at him. "How do I know you're telling me the truth now?"

He returned her look steadily, but she almost thought she saw him wince a bit. "You were the one who figured it out," he reminded her.

True, she thought. But for some reason she couldn't let go of the idea. Who had told whom what? Trying to rerun their conversation from earlier, she realized she might have given him more information about his identity than he had given her.

Maybe she had fed him a story to use. What if he was a member of some terrorist group and…

Stop it. There she was again, asking too many questions, being suspicious of everything. She had seen the article that said Kenneth Maxwell had joined the ATF. He had told her his real name, hadn't he?

But something in her face must have reached him. He let go of her hand and stood. His eyes had become polar again.

"I told you more of the truth than I've told anyone I don't work with," he said shortly. "You'll believe what you choose to believe. But from here on out, Liza, stay away from me. You could get me killed. Or I could get you killed. So just stay the hell away."

Then he was gone, closing the door quietly behind him. But she hadn't missed the pain that had flickered over his face.

God, she had done it again.

Max roared away from Liza's apartment feeling like an open wound. How could she believe him? Well, that was the question, wasn't it, when your life was a total lie.

As his bike gobbled up miles of narrow country road, he faced his damn demons again. He lived a lie. He had to live a lie. He protected people by living a lie.

For God's sake, what that group he'd just been involved with intended to do... Even if he had stopped only one of their plans from being executed, he had saved hundreds of lives. Lives that would have been torn and shattered by bombs. He surely didn't need to apologize for that.

But the doubts that had begun plaguing him months ago remained. He not only lied to others, but he lied to himself. He had to. He needed to believe his own lies in order to function. He had to become what he was pretending to be. Deep inside, some tiny kernel of him remembered that it was all an act, but the act became overwhelmingly real. Because it had to, in order to work.

At times he'd felt adrift inside himself, felt as if he were losing touch with the guy who had joined the ATF. Lately he'd wondered if the case had gone on longer if he would have totally lost touch. He wouldn't have been the first undercover agent to become who he was pretending to be.

Cognitive dissonance, the shrink had called it when they pulled him out after the arrests. You say something often enough, do things often enough, and the mind starts to fall in line. You start believing the bull because you're saying it and living it.

So maybe Liza was right to question who he really was. He wasn't sure he knew himself.

And that was the hell of it. A name was meaningless. It held no intrinsic reality. Reality was what went on inside you. What had been going on inside him for too long was not stuff he would identify with Ken Maxwell.

He knew one thing for certain, though: he was never going under again. Never. He was burned out so badly that he'd muffed it with Liza right from the start. He couldn't do it anymore.

Something deep inside him was rebelling, demanding to be allowed to find some level of reality that wouldn't have to change again. Some truth of identity that could remain stable.

And damn it, he was getting sick of being alone inside himself. He needed some enduring connections with people he wasn't hoping to send to jail. It had been nearly a decade since he'd even allowed himself a girlfriend, because he couldn't get involved with his subjects, and he couldn't drag an innocent woman into his life.

He was sick of one-night stands with women just to satisfy his physical needs, or worse yet, to prove he was okay to some meathead.

He was sick of not being able to share life or himself with anyone in a meaningful way.

Why wouldn't Liza wonder if he was telling the truth now? He'd started with lies, giving her no reason to trust him.

So who was Kenneth Maxwell, he wondered? Neither the darkness, nor the road, offered answers.

But then, just as he was heading back into town, a long-buried memory flashed up before his eyes and he almost went off the road.

Just before he'd been welcomed into the militia's inner circle, he'd been invited to a meeting. And what he saw was the stuff of nightmares. A woman had confided something about the group to someone she shouldn't have talked to. And her body lay there at the center of the camp, staked out, obviously tortured, a warning to everyone about what happened to people who had loose lips.

Yeah, he knew what these guys were capable of. It had been all he could do not to blow the lid right then. But he hadn't seen what had happened, he didn't have the evidence he'd been sent in to get and he'd have ruined the entire operation, setting it back years and maybe costing innocent lives.

So he'd swallowed his anger and buried the memory because he had to. Silence, though, had made him complicit.

Well, not exactly silence. He'd gotten word back to

Ames, and Ames had told him to let it rest until they rolled up the operation.

Suddenly he jammed on his brakes, leaving rubber on the pavement. At the side of the road, he sat staring into darkness, feeling his gorge rise, and wondering just how different he really was from the guys he was after.

The night didn't have any answers for that, either. All he knew for sure anymore was that he lived, breathed and existed to put the rest of those creeps in jail forever.

But even that wouldn't absolve him.

Liza sat hugging a pillow, hoping Max would come back but knowing he wouldn't. Why would he? If he hadn't been telling the truth, he'd want to stay away. If he had, then she had just offended him beyond belief.

She'd done it again. What was the quirk that led her to question everything, even after she had thought the questions were settled?

It was poisoning her life.

She seemed to be incapable of accepting all but the most inconsequential things at face value.

Once that had been a good thing. In her former job, it had given her an edge. But she was no longer a reporter, and what had been a useful gift then might have become a serious liability.

It had certainly driven people out of her life. Did she want that to continue?

Dang. She looked at her computer, feeling the old itch to resume her search, to look for some concrete proof that the man with whom she had just shared an incredible sexual experience was exactly who he said he was.

And realizing in an instant that resuming her search was the worst thing she could do.

If he was telling the truth—

She drew herself up short. If? If? Was she going to do that again?

The itch was strong, compelling. Almost compulsive. But if what he had told her was true, it could be dangerous to him, and possibly to her. And if he was lying, what would she find anyway? Little enough as she'd already discovered.

Groaning, she flopped back on the couch, holding the pillow tight. Maybe it was time to give up her self-image as a reporter, and become an ordinary human being.

The kind who wasn't suspicious of every damn thing. The kind who could accept things at face value until events proved them wrong.

But even as she was thinking that she needed to learn new behaviors, she wondered if it had ever really been about her "nose for news." Maybe her curiosity had its roots in something else.

Staring up at her ceiling, she wondered exactly where she had learned not to trust.

And why.

Chapter 6

"It's not easy going undercover," Gage said to Max over coffee at the sheriff's office. The sun was barely above the horizon, but some things couldn't wait on the business day. One of them was coffee.

"I was surprised to find you here already," Max remarked.

"I gotta get here before Velma. It's the only way I can make sure my first coffee of the day isn't toxic mud."

Max smiled faintly. "She's a dragon."

"A good dragon." Gage sighed and motioned to the burn scars on his face. "You know what happened?"

Max shook his head.

"Car bomb. I made a mistake. I never thought the drug dealers would figure out where I lived. But they did, somehow, and they tried to get me. They got my first wife and kids instead."

Max swore. "How do you live with that?"

"Like I said, it isn't easy. I knew a cop from Arizona, I think it was. He went under for eight years. So deep that only one other cop knew who he was. He was so damn good at it that he got arrested regularly, and beaten up by the cops more than once. When it was over, he got all kinds of medals and apologies, and then he walked away. I don't know what he did after that, but he had no interest in being a cop anymore."

"I'm almost there myself."

Gage nodded. "Living lies isn't easy unless you're a sociopath or psychotic or something. But that's what deep cover makes us do. I'm not surprised you're starting to wonder who you are, and I'm even less surprised that you're reaching the end of the line on it."

Max didn't say anything. He'd turned to Gage, his one local contact who knew the truth, a man who had a similar experience and background in the DEA, in the hopes he could find some pearl of wisdom. All he was hearing was a reflection of his own thoughts.

Gage sighed and leaned forward, wincing a bit. "So Liza has it figured out."

"Yeah, and what she didn't figure out I basically told her. She has the agency scrambling, and we're all worried someone might connect her with me. It's remote, but it's possible."

Gage touched his cheek again. "It's possible, all right. And just when we start thinking it isn't, it happens."

"Was she always this curious?"

Gage shrugged. "She's been away for a while. I do seem to remember she was serious and awfully determined. I guess having your dad build a boat in the backyard when there isn't any sailing water for hundreds of miles teaches you something about determination."

"Yeah." The word came out on a short laugh.

Gage smiled crookedly. "I hope you don't want my advice. Because I don't have any. I remember that feeling of being at sea when I was undercover. Oh, initially it didn't bother me much, but there comes a point where it starts to get too real. I touched base with my family from time to time and it helped keep me centered. And just when I thought it was all over, I learned it wasn't."

Max tensed a bit. "You're telling me to be on guard."

"I'm telling you that until the last criminal is behind bars, you need to watch your back. And now you need to watch Liza's, too. I'm glad you told me about her, because now I can keep an eye out. But regardless of how mixed-up you may be feeling about everything, you've got as much of a duty right now as you had all along."

"To protect."

"Bingo."

"I already knew that."

"I know." Another crooked smile.

"So basically you're telling me to give up the Hamlet gig for now?"

That elicited a laugh from Gage. "I guess I am. For the time being. God knows I spent years sorting out who I was, who I am and who I wanted to be. It's a fact most of us actually spend our entire lives doing exactly that. We just don't see it so starkly."

"But how do you live with the other stuff?"

Gage paused, mug halfway to his mouth. "You mean that line we're never supposed to cross, the one that we sometimes cross anyway? The one that leaves us wondering if we're any better than they are?"

Max nodded.

"Damned if I know. Putting them away helps a little. Time helps more, once you get back to the clean side of the fence."

That bit about his duty stuck with Max as he rode his bike over to Maude's, picked up two breakfasts that smelled good enough to make his mouth water and headed back to Liza's.

He was damn nervous, wondering if she would even open the door to him.

But the bottom line was, he had to figure out a way to protect her.

And he also had to lay down some ground rules before they both got themselves killed.

Liza climbed out of a shower after a restless night. With a towel wrapped around her wet hair, she tied the belt of a sage-green terry cloth robe and went to check the peephole.

Her heart slammed when she saw Max. She'd lain awake half the night tormented by the heart-crushing certainty that he would avoid her like the plague now, and the equal certainty that there was something very wrong with her.

But there he was. Her hands fumbled as she turned the dead bolt and opened the door.

"Hi," he said and lifted two white food boxes topped by a brown paper bag. "Breakfast, if you'll let me in."

Astonishment combined with suspicion as she opened the door wider.

"Bad time?" he asked as she closed the door. He eyed her towel and robe. "Unfortunately, this is hot. Can you eat with that towel on your head?"

"I can try," she said, then cleared her throat when she heard her own froggy croak.

"Good." He marched over to the table and set one box on each side. "I brought plastic utensils so you won't have to wash a thing." Out of the bag he pulled two tall cups. "Coffee. I hope you like Maude's lattes."

"I do," she admitted, coming cautiously closer. "To what do I owe this honor?"

"I feel bad about the way I left last night. Plus, I was reminded of something important."

Finally she dared to meet his eyes. The polar blue looked a little warmer now than last night. "And that was?"

"That regardless of how you got ensnared in my messy life, I still have a duty to protect you."

She dropped into one of the chairs, a bit over-whelmed and startled. "A duty to protect me?" That sounded, well, awfully strong. It also wasn't what she wanted from him. In fact, it annoyed her.

"It's true." He sat facing her and handed her a set of plastic-wrapped utensils and a couple of paper napkins. Early-morning sunlight started to find its way through the nearby window, turning the room golden.

"But there's no evidence I'm in danger."

"Doesn't matter." He slipped his jacket off, letting it trail over the back of his chair, revealing yet another of his black T-shirts. "I spent a lot of years protecting people I'll never meet. It was my job…it was my duty. You're part of that duty now."

"I can take care of myself."

"Ordinarily I'd agree with you. But you don't know these guys. So, respectfully, I have to disagree this time. What I'm suggesting here is that we reach an understanding that will be helpful to us both."

"I don't want to be anyone's duty."

The corners of his eyes crinkled just a bit. "I'm sure

you don't. Then there's reality. Don't let your food get cold."

She opened the box and found hash browns, scrambled eggs and a slice of ham. The aromas that reached her made her instantly hungry. She ripped open the plastic and took out a fork. "Thanks for breakfast. And what do you mean by reality?"

He hesitated. "Do you know Gage Dalton's story?"

"I think everyone in the county does."

"Then you know how innocent people can get swept into a mess like this. However remote it may seem, it can happen. If someone links you to me, and me to my recent alias, you could be caught up in it, Liza. I'd be derelict if I ignored the possibility."

"Derelict, huh?" The word didn't seem to fit him at all.

"Derelict," he repeated. "So whether you like it or not, I feel a duty here. Thus, we need ground rules."

Her stomach knotted a bit and she put her fork down. "I already quit looking into your background. I won't do anything at all that might draw attention to you."

"It might be too late."

The knot in her stomach tightened. She wanted to argue, but he'd deprived her of arguments when he mentioned Gage. He was absolutely right—there was no guarantee that no one other than his bosses would make the connections he was worried about.

"How do we do this?" she asked finally. "I'm not inclined to...trust easily." It hurt to admit it, especially since that distrust extended well beyond her job. If it hadn't, from the moment she had met Max McKenny she would have simply accepted him as another instructor.

He stood up and shoved his hand into the back

pocket of his jeans. He pulled out a slim leather case and put it on the table in front of her.

"Try this," he said.

She reached out and flipped the case open. There was no mistaking the badge or the ID card right beside it. She had seen them before, and recognized them. Unless she wanted to claim this was a top-of-the-line forgery, the truth lay right before her eyes.

He had resumed his seat and started eating, apparently waiting for her response.

"I'm sorry," she said, hearing the tension in her own voice.

"For what?"

"For not believing you."

"I don't even believe myself anymore. Why would you?" He gave an almost invisible shrug, but she sensed that that truly disturbed him. Which only made her feel even worse.

"Look, Max," she said, forcing the words out, "I realized last night that I've become entirely too untrusting for my own good. I thought it was part of being a good reporter, but maybe it's some character flaw that got enhanced by my job. I don't know. But I'm sorry. If I'd only believed from the beginning that you were just another teacher, we wouldn't be here right now."

"No, we wouldn't," he agreed bluntly.

She flushed, and not just because he was right. Memories of what had happened between them last night kept leaping up, tormenting her. Apparently that was to be put firmly in the past and forgotten. So much the better, she tried to tell herself.

He continued speaking. "Okay, then. So here we are. When I said ground rules, I didn't mean I was going to lay down the law. I meant we need to collaborate on ways to help keep you safe if these nuts do make the connection. Can you live with that?"

A blast of arctic air would still have been welcome, especially as the heat in her face immediately poured downward to pool between her legs. Her body knew exactly what it wanted even if her brain was all mixed-up. She shifted a bit in her chair, trying to ease the heaviness of desire.

"I can live with that," she agreed, hating the huskiness in her voice. Damn, she needed some self-control in more ways than one. "Where do you suggest we start?"

"We start with trust. You can't work a job like this without it. You have to trust me and I have to trust you."

"This is a job?" Considering what she was feeling, she didn't much like that description.

"Yes."

Her cheeks heated again and she damned her pale skin. God, he could drive her nuts so fast it was beyond belief. One second she wanted him, and the next she wanted to throttle him.

"We have to trust each other, Liza. Because if something starts to come down, there's going to be no time for questions or argument. Can you trust me?"

"I can try." She nodded toward the badge case. "That was a good start."

"Good."

"Now what?"

He smiled. "For right now, let's eat and you can ask me any questions you want. I promise to answer you truthfully, and if I can't answer for some operational reason, I'll say so flat out. No deflection. No equivocation."

"Can you do that?"

She watched his face as she waited for his response. She saw shadows pass, and pain.

"Look," he said, "the truth is I'm a consummate liar."

"Like that old joke, a drug dealer is honest while a narc can never be."

"You've heard that one, too."

She nodded, biting her lower lip.

"Well, it's true," he admitted. "And I'd be lying if I said it hasn't affected me. I've been living a lie for years. Everything I said, thought, did—all of it had to line up with the role. I had to believe my own lies so I wouldn't trip up."

"That has to be hard."

"It's worse than hard. It's a self-inflicted wound."

Her heart squeezed with pain for him. She had never, ever thought of that.

"My sense of self is a tangled mess. One thing I know for certain, I am absolutely done with working undercover. If you want the truth, I feel like somebody put me through a blender and I'm picking up the pieces trying to decide which belong to Max and which belong to not-Max."

"My God, that's awful."

"It's not fun. But I chose to do this job, so now I have to see it through. Send those guys to jail and put myself back together. So I'm going to start by being as honest with you as I can, okay?"

She nodded.

"So where's that famous curiosity? The book is open for your exploration."

The odd thing was, right now she didn't have any questions. All she had was a whole lot of sympathy for Max. "I'm still trying to absorb this. I got so mad at you for lying to me, and now I've got to deal with what that lying did to you. I never considered the ramifications."

"Why would you? Everything glamorizes going undercover, from TV to novels. Nobody looks at the ugly side."

"Does everyone have these problems?"

"Enough that the agency has a number of psychologists and shrinks to help with reentry. And that's what it is—reentry. Some get really high on going undercover and do it as long as they can. Others start to find it increasingly difficult and want to get out. I guess in that respect I was the wrong person for the job."

"Oh, don't say that. Maybe you just need to be you again."

"If I can find me."

She hesitated, reminding herself that she really didn't know him all that well, but one of his statements had really stuck with her. "Kenneth Maxwell is a guy who joined the ATF so that other people wouldn't suffer like his mother did."

He grew utterly still then nodded slowly. "That's who he used to be. I wonder if he still is."

"I'm sure he is. After all, he's here right now talking about a duty to protect me when I may have just caused him a major headache."

But he didn't look as if that was any help. His gaze held painful memories. "You don't know what I've done, Liza," he reminded her. "And there's a whole bunch I'll never tell you."

She pulled back into her shell, taking the warning to heart. She was right to be afraid of her attraction to him. He'd just as good as told her so. Maybe she wasn't crazy to be so distrusting.

She looked down at her plate, deciding that a badge

only meant he was a cop, that it didn't mean anything else at all. Certainly not that she should trust him with anything more than her physical safety.

Maybe she should hang on to her cloak of emotional armor a little longer.

"Anyway," he said after a little while, "my self-doubts are seriously self-indulgent right now."

"Why?"

"Because we have more important things to consider than my splintered personality. Like what to teach you about awareness and self-protection. The short course in how to be an agent."

The thought chilled her a bit, but she tried for a joke anyway. "Given my naturally suspicious nature, that shouldn't be too hard."

His smile was fleeting. "I hope not."

She hesitated. "Seriously, how likely is it that anyone could make the link between us and who you were?"

"Seriously? I'd have said it's totally unlikely. But it's the things you don't prepare for that bite you in the butt. The more people who know who I am, the more likely it is that someone will let the cat out of the bag."

"So how many know?"

"Your sheriff for one. You. My handler. A number of people at the bureau and in the U.S. Attorney's office. I can't give you exact numbers, but the more I thought about it last night, the more nervous I got. Each person who knows increases the risk. I can't ignore that."

He was right about that. As a reporter, the natural desire of people to share what they knew had been her meat and potatoes for a long time.

"People aren't good at keeping secrets," she said. "And the more secret something is, the more likely it is that they'll want to share it, simply to puff up their own importance. Leaks are the rule rather than the exception. I've had people tell me the most incredible things on background."

He nodded. "I'd like to say that it's different in the agency, but people are people."

"All you need is one person who doesn't like you, or one person who needs to feel important." She pushed her breakfast aside, her appetite gone. "I hate to tell you how many of them I ran into in my job."

"Maybe that's why you find it hard to trust. You met too many untrustworthy people."

"Could be. God knows, I was swimming in them. It's not like some of them didn't have good reasons for giving me information. Despite what a lot of people think, public servants do care about getting the job done right. Some of them, anyway. They care enough to risk their careers by coming to someone like me with information."

"Blowing my identity won't enhance anyone's job prospects."

She gathered he was trying to sound encouraging, but she didn't feel encouraged. She knew too many of the other kind, people who felt insignificant or who believed they had a grievance. Way too many.

All of a sudden the possibility that someone might reveal Max's whereabouts didn't seem so unlikely.

"You know," she said slowly, "if someone wants to blow your cover, I may have given them the cover they need."

He appeared to think about it. "It's possible."

"Well, it could be blamed on my nosing around. Why would they look anywhere else?"

"You really do have a suspicious mind."

Even though she could hear no criticism in his tone,

it angered her anyway. She jumped up from the table and caught the damp towel as it fell from her head.

"All right," she snapped. "I'm suspicious. That doesn't mean I'm always wrong."

"No, it doesn't. I just hadn't considered that possibility. And you might be right."

She refused to be mollified. Bad enough that she'd lost the job she loved and had to adjust to a new life, but now this man had caused her to question herself in ways that provided no answers. It was as if the last foundation had been torn from beneath her.

She circled the room, half-formed angry statements buzzing around in her mind, absolutely none of them useful or even appropriate.

"Liza, I'm sorry. I didn't mean that critically."

She knew he hadn't, but the echoes of other times and other men remained. And now those things that before had merely angered her also hurt.

"Liza." Strong arms wound around her, stilling her, and cradled her close to a hard chest. "Liza," he said again.

She pushed away, not ready for comfort or his touch. Tossing the towel over her shoulder, she said, "I'm going to get dressed."

Because she didn't want to spill her pain. She hardly knew this guy, and didn't want to expose herself that way. Not yet. She had to trust him about some things, but she didn't have to trust him with her feelings.

In her small bedroom, she donned jeans, a flannel shirt and some boots. She ran a brush impatiently through her damp hair and then clipped it, still wet, to the back of her head. She didn't even bother with makeup.

She needed to get out of here, get away and blow off

steam somehow. Just as she thought she was becoming resigned to things the way they were, she discovered she wasn't resigned to anything at all. Not in the least.

She was astonished to find that Max was still there.

"Let's blow this joint," he said with a crooked smile. "We can get on my bike and ride hell for leather, or anything else you feel like."

"You don't have to hover over me."

His smile faded. "Yes, Liza, I do."

Oh, she hated that. Hated that she couldn't honestly argue with him. She'd seen enough of the underside over the years to know that there might really be a threat. And she knew people. Which was the main reason she found it so hard to trust.

There it was: the answer to her question. She'd learned not to trust because she had met too many untrustworthy people, including boyfriends.

She swore silently.

"What do you want to do, Liza?"

"I want to be mad and frustrated and hate the world."

"I can handle that."

But the sound of her own words made her feel childish, and her anger fizzled a bit. "I want to walk," she said finally, grabbing for her jacket on the hook by the door.

"Okay. Here or someplace else?"

"Here is fine." She slipped her jacket on, grabbed her keys and wallet and opened the door.

Max was right behind her, his jacket slung over his shoulder, hanging on his index finger. They strode down her hallway, down the stairs and out into a world drenched in the buttery light of autumn. The air felt crisp and fresh and Liza drew it deeply into her lungs.

She strode at a rapid pace for about five blocks, but

then began to slow to a steadier and easier walk. Her ire and upset eased. Gradually she grew aware of the beauty of the day, and of the man who kept pace beside her.

"I didn't mean to upset you," Max said as they rounded a corner onto a tree-lined street brightened by the fall colors. Brilliant golds and oranges had begun to dominate as the trees gave up their summer cloaks.

"It's been a tough year," she said, "and I think I'm being too sensitive."

"I was trying to compliment you."

She shoved her hands into her pockets and stopped to face him. "Maybe so. It's just hard for me to take it that way anymore."

"The ex-boyfriend?"

"Yeah." She resumed walking because she did not want to look at him. Especially when she couldn't ignore that pull of sexual attraction. It wasn't helping to sort anything out for her.

"Most of my relationships broke up because guys couldn't stand my unreliability. I lost track of the times I had to cancel a date because I was in the midst of some story with a deadline to meet. About the third time you do that, they start looking for someone who leads a normal life."

"Okay."

"But there was this one guy. I fell really hard, and he didn't seem to mind my chaotic life. But he got really irritated by my curiosity and questions. He said it was like being given the third degree all the time." She would never forget when he'd accused her in a mocking voice of demanding to know exactly what color the sky was. "He said if I couldn't get over being so damn suspicious, he wasn't going to be able to take it."

"Ouch."

"Yeah, ouch. So I tried hard not to question him beyond very casual things like how his day had gone. Which started making me feel tense because we weren't having a real conversation anymore. See, another of my hangups."

"I don't think that's a hangup. He wasn't letting you be you."

"That thought crossed my mind, but since he wasn't the first to comment on my inquisitorial nature, I took it to heart."

"And more so because you really cared about him. So what happened?"

"I'd love to tell you I left him because he tried to change me. But the truth is, I pulled into this tight little shell and stopped questioning him about anything. And then I found out why he hated my questions so much."

"Why?"

"His wife called me."

He was silent a moment. "His wife?"

The memory still put a spear through her heart.

"Liza," he said presently, "after that, I'd be surprised if you weren't suspicious."

"Well, yeah, but it wasn't just that. It's a whole bunch of things. Reporters have to take almost no one at their word. As the saying about sources goes, 'If your mother tells you she loves you, check it out.'"

"God, no wonder you did a background check on me. And I'm amazed that you're not furious with me for lying to you."

"You at least seem to have a legitimate reason for it."

At that a small laugh escaped him. "I seem to," he pointed out.

"Yeah, seem," she admitted. "That's my problem,

and like I said, it didn't all come about because of Craig. He wasn't the first and he wasn't the last to find me too inquisitive. He just made it worse."

They continued to walk in silence while she struggled internally, wondering why she had told him so much, inevitably wondering if the story was safe with him.

Astonishment hit her when she realized that she wanted to trust Max McKenny, Kenneth Maxwell, whoever he was. This past week hadn't been about reasonable suspicion but rather about her fear that she couldn't trust a man. So she'd sought a reason to distrust him.

"Whoa," she said, stopping dead in her tracks.

"What?" he asked.

She shook her head and started walking again. She wasn't ready to share that bit of self-understanding. Perhaps she never would be. "So what's this about teaching me how to be an agent?"

"It's all about shifting gears," he said. "For example, when you're walking down the street, you need to be aware of everyone and everything, not woolgathering."

Remembering the day she had walked right into him on campus, she had to admit he had a point. "Okay." She lifted her head a little higher and started looking around, taking in the day and the unpopulated street.

"How well do you know the town and most of the people here?"

"Well, I used to know everyone, but that was a long time ago. There are new people, but I think I've begun to recognize most of them. And I'm getting so I know most of our student body by sight."

"It's not a large student body," he agreed. "I recognize them, too, even if I don't know who they are. Okay, so first thing is to notice anyone you don't recognize or who seems out of place."

"Like you."

He laughed at that, and she was finally able to smile. "Maybe you were born with the talent," he said.

Maybe she was, because a lot of what he told her during the rest of their walk seemed intuitively obvious: be on the alert for strangers, people who seemed too interested in her, people who might be following her, and avoid getting too close to places where people could hide.

She felt pleasantly relaxed by the time they returned to her apartment, energized by the walk and the weather and the feeling that she had learned something very important about herself. And nothing about "heightened awareness" seemed particularly onerous.

Except her heightened awareness of him. He made no move to leave, and she couldn't figure out if it was because he wanted to spend time with her or was just doing his "duty."

That was annoying, she decided as she made a pot of coffee. It wasn't a question that was going to leave her alone, but she found herself reluctant to ask. Maybe because she was afraid of what he would say.

"We'll go over to the gym when you've got the time," he remarked. "I need to teach you some basic self-defense moves."

"Okay." She wouldn't mind learning a few of those.

But self-defense was far from the uppermost thing in her mind. She couldn't settle now, and the relaxation she had felt upon their return seemed to be slipping away. She was hyperaware of him, of the way he filled her apartment, of what had passed between them only last night.

She turned her back to look out her window, trying to find her center. Too many things were coming at her too fast, and while she'd always believed she thrived on that as a reporter, this was different. This was her life.

"Liza?"

She turned and saw him pat the couch where he was sitting. "Talk to me?" he asked.

She hesitated, then went to sit beside him, leaving a few safe inches between them. He smelled so good that she almost edged away even farther. Then she caught herself.

"What's wrong?"

The question proved to be unanswerable. For once she had nothing to say, nothing to ask. His very presence stymied her. She was swimming in doubt, desire and even a little fear.

"I'm sorry," he said when she remained quiet. "I've really sandbagged you, haven't I?"

Well, that was one way of looking at it, she thought. He'd come out of the blue, made her review her own character and life, had awakened a desire she didn't really want and now was making her wonder if he was there because he felt it was his duty or because he wanted to be with her. Never mind the stuff about how she might be in danger. She didn't really believe that, not yet. Even though it was possible.

But all of this was totally out of her experience.

She ordinarily thrived on new experiences, risks, excitement. But right now she felt as if she was floundering in emotional quicksand.

She wished she could shake herself and make things settle down.

It had been a tough year, but nothing unique had happened to her. Nothing that didn't happen to thousands of people all the time, so she didn't want to use that as an excuse.

Nor was it. The things troubling her right now had nothing to do with losing a job she loved and undertaking a new one that she mostly enjoyed. But her identity had shattered when she turned in her press card, and that made her think about how and why she had come to let a job define her.

Which at least gave her something to say to Max before he started asking about her silence.

"I let my job define me. Do you suppose most people do that?"

"I did," he admitted. "I guess I still do to some extent."

"But that's not a whole person."

"No, it's not. I'm living proof of that."

She finally looked at him. "So why do we do that? Why do we define ourselves by our actions? Human doings instead of human beings?"

His eyebrows lifted. "One thing I know I'm not is a philosopher."

"Me, either."

"So what brought this on?"

She shrugged. There was no way to explain the conflicting emotions he aroused in her. No way at all.

He astonished her then by lifting one arm and drawing her close to his side. "That's not part of the job," he said, then added, "I like it, Liza. I like holding you."

He'd arrowed straight to part of her concerns again, making her wonder if she was an open book. But she liked his arm around her, liked being pressed to his side, so she relaxed against him and let him hold her.

"It's been years since I've spent time with a woman like you," he remarked.

"What do you mean?"

"Let's just say my choices were dictated by circumstances and an unwillingness to drag some innocent into my life."

She considered all the things he might mean by that, and none of them sounded good to her. "So no relationships?"

"Not real ones. And nothing that ever lasted very long. I couldn't afford it. And I couldn't risk someone by becoming involved."

"I can see that." But she had trouble imagining how that had made him feel. "Going undercover is ugly, isn't it."

"Yes." His answer was uncompromising.

She turned a little so she could look at him. "But it's necessary, Max. Somebody has to do it. There's so much bad that would happen without people like you."

"That's what I tell myself. It's certainly true of my last operation. But it's still ugly."

Feeling a pang for him she turned enough to wrap her arm around his waist. "I think you should be proud of yourself."

"Maybe someday. Right now I have too much time to think. When I saw you walking toward me at the faculty tea, I should have run."

She looked up at him. "Why?"

"Because my instincts warned me you were trouble. But I just stood there, utterly captivated."

Captivated? She liked the sound of that.

He twisted a bit so they were almost facing each other. "I was rooted on the spot by a fantastic figure and cat-green eyes. I watched you coming and I didn't want to get out of the way."

Tension inside her began to ease as she read honesty

in his face. So what if he was by his own admission a consummate liar? He couldn't fake that heat in his gaze.

A warm wave of need washed through her, and suddenly none of the rest of it mattered.

He seemed to read the response in her face leaning toward her, his intent clear. And for once she didn't bother to question anything—not what he was doing, not what she was doing—because it felt so right.

His mouth found hers gently this time, as if he were giving her a chance to back away. Or as if, after last night, he was sure of his welcome and willing to take time.

Kiss after gentle kiss dropped on her lips, and his hand came to cradle the back of her head, holding her close and steadying her.

No one, she realized, had ever kissed her like this before. Never. The lightest touches of their mouths, like a soft caress, as if he were delicately seeking nectar among the petals of her lips.

Her response, however, was as electric as anything she'd ever felt. Those light brushes soon had her hungry for more. She could have wrapped her arms around him and demanded it, but instead she chose to wait, enjoying the anticipation with every cell of her body.

She slid her fingers into his hair, enjoying the texture, as her senses filled with him. She couldn't ever remember noticing a man's scent before. Max smelled of soap, fresh air and a hint of musk that delighted her. Just as heady as his scent was the power she could feel in his muscles.

And his mouth. Oh, his delightful mouth, tasting of coffee as he speared his tongue into her at last. With slow, sinuous movements, he tangled their tongues together, teasing and tormenting all at once.

"You taste so sweet," he whispered huskily, then kissed her so deeply she felt it all the way to her toes. He slipped his arm under her legs and draped them over his lap, holding her even closer.

His hand slid up along her thigh, awakening a whole new area of nerve endings, then continued its teasing climb until at last he cupped her breast.

"Perfect," he whispered as she gasped in pleasure.

No one had ever claimed anything about her was perfect, but the thought faded in a new wave of desire as he kneaded her until her nipple pebbled. Then his thumb began to brush it, driving her nearly insane.

"Max…" She could barely gasp his name as he trailed his tongue along the sensitive column of her throat. He answered by pinching her nipple and sending a sizzling arc of pleasure straight to her center where she throbbed. She wouldn't have believed she could groan from such a simple touch. But she did.

That evidently pleased him, for he pinched her a little harder, causing her to writhe against him and clamp her thighs together. Then, almost before she realized it, he slipped his hand up under her shirt and bra, and claimed her naked breast.

The sensation was exquisite, like fire, and the heat and roughness of his palm on her unprotected skin filled her with yearning for more. Her response to his touch was momentous, as if in all her life before she had barely peeked at what was possible.

She felt him start to slide her shirt up, and delicious anticipation filled her, lifting her halfway to the stars, driving the rest of the world to some far corner of the universe.

Every cell in her body sang "Yesss!"

Then his cell phone rang.

Chapter 7

It was a good thing Liza had been around the block a time or three, or she might have been utterly shocked by the word that escaped Max as he abruptly drew away and reached in his back pocket for his phone.

"I'm sorry," he said, meeting her gaze before he pressed the talk button and answered. "Max."

He'd stopped for a cell phone call? That might have ticked her off except that it suddenly struck her passion-clouded mind that he probably received calls from only one place or person on that line. Just as she had always known it was an editor when her business cell had rung. There were some calls you didn't ignore.

Just another of those things that had put a damper on her romantic life. He was listening intently and looking more serious by the minute, so she sat up, took her legs off his lap and adjusted her shirt and bra.

He didn't say much, just muttered agreement into

the phone. She went to get the coffeepot, sniffed it and decided to reheat it.

As she was starting it, she heard Max enter the kitchen behind her. "Coffee?" she asked, feeling unusually nervous and reluctant to look at him. Maybe one of these days she needed to learn how to say no to Max. Because it occurred to her she was rolling over entirely too easily to his advances. Before she'd always made men wait. Wanted to get to really know them. Not that that caution had saved her much grief evidently.

"Sure," he said.

Something in his tone forced her to turn and look at him. "Bad news?" she asked, ignoring a sudden thumping of her heart.

"Maybe. My handler says it appears somebody has found out who I really am."

She studied him, took in the angles and planes of his face, the way his icy blue eyes looked almost sharp and the way the corners of them seemed tight. "Max?"

"Yeah?"

"How could they get from whatever alias you used to your real name? I mean, wouldn't that connection be even more buried than you are here?"

"I thought I was pretty well buried here," he said, one corner of his mouth lifting humorlessly. "You penetrated this ID."

"But your old— What do you call them anyway, the group you were infiltrating?"

"Subs. Subjects."

"They didn't know you were a lawyer, did they? I mean, that's the trail I followed, and your guys almost had me dead-ended."

"I don't know," he said flatly. "They were supposed to think I went to jail with the others to await trial.

Those we arrested have been kept separate. It's the usual way to protect people like me. Somebody must have figured out I'm not in jail."

"But even then, it's not like the ATF publicly lists its agents. Do they?"

"No." He shook his head. "But I think I told you these guys have got one hell of a hacker. I suppose they figured they were busted by an agent, not just someone from a neighboring town. In fact, that would be a likely conclusion, given the way it came down."

She poured them both fresh coffee and they returned to the living room. She sat on the couch, but he paced, holding his mug, clearly running a whole bunch of stuff through his head.

"What kind of group were they exactly?" she asked.

"They were just the right blend of political and religious fanaticism to worry us. A group of true believers who could find the numbers six-six-six in just about anything. The main core was surrounded by a lot of folks who were almost innocent by comparison. They didn't know the true purpose of what the leaders planned, but they were soaking up enough propaganda and brainwashing to become useful tools at the right time."

"I've seen things like that before."

"What we had was a militant cult that wanted to overthrow the government as part of their master plan for bringing about the end times."

"I don't see the connection."

"Most end-timers are waiting for the fall of Israel. A handful are even trying to make it happen, because it's part of the prediction. These guys had managed to transfer the apocalyptic predictions to this country. Don't ask me how—it took me a couple of years to get all the connections straight and I'm still not exactly sure what the highest leadership actually believed. It may just have been what they were selling."

She nodded. "I've more than once wondered if the head honcho believed his own marketing."

"Exactly. Anyway, you don't need to know more than that."

Those words were crystal clear to her. He couldn't tell her, and she had to respect that, as much as she would have loved to pick his brain for every detail.

"Okay," she said, and sipped her coffee. "So it took you years to get in?"

"These guys are paranoid. So I had to hang around the fringes, get to know some of the guys at bars and on a local firing range. Gradually I got deeper, met more people. I have a useful knowledge of guns. I know how to build bombs. I let this out a bit at a time, as if I was showing off for friends. Then I started talking the party line little by little as if they were persuading me." He stopped. "Anyway, I got to the center of the group after a couple of years. Then I had to get in with the guys who really count. That was actually the hard part."

"I bet." She was fascinated, hoping he'd tell her more.

For a while he said nothing, then added, "After eighteen months at the apex, I had passed on enough information to get them. Unfortunately, a handful of them didn't show up at the meeting we raided."

"And you think those folks are after you."

"I don't think it, I know it. I'm the primary witness. I'm the one who is going to back up all the hard evidence with my testimony about who, where, when and what. Without me, it falls apart. Or could be picked apart."

He suddenly stopped pacing and turned to her. "Listen, I gotta get out of here. Want to come?"

She didn't even ask where. She could understand the need to get out and just move while you worked things through in your head. She'd had to do that sometimes when she was working on a particularly difficult or gritty story. There were times when she had wondered if she was going to leave a rut eventually as she paced the streets of downtown St. Petersburg.

Outside, dressed against the chill, they mounted his motorcycle. As they drove the residential streets he kept to the speed limit, but as soon as they hit the mountain roads, he accelerated to dizzying speeds.

She realized then that he was a born risk taker. But wouldn't he have to be? She was, too, and as the adrenaline began to surge in response to the tight hairpin turns on the narrow mountain roads, exhilaration filled her.

She clung to his back, enjoying the pounding of her heart, the closeness to him, the speed that added to the thrill. But she couldn't shake her concern for him.

So his handlers thought someone might be getting close to finding out who he was. But whoever was looking for him was coming from a different direction than she had been. She had picked up the trail from the end, a far easier task, she thought, than picking it up from the beginning.

She wondered what he was thinking, what he was deciding and whether he'd be gone by nightfall.

After all, he was only renting a motel room. He could leave at any time, and someone like Gage could step in to take over his course. Or maybe his bosses could send someone to take his place. The term had hardly begun, though, and it wasn't past the point where they could just cancel the class until next semester.

So he could leave. The thought deadened the thrill she felt as they took another tight turn with a gorge so close and deep she had no trouble imagining them going over the edge.

But Max knew what he was doing with the bike and the tires didn't even squeal. She lost track of where they were, knew only that they were zigzagging ever higher into the mountains. Leaving demons behind, she thought. Except as she knew all too well, demons could seldom be left behind.

But the adrenaline rush and the speed felt good to her, and they probably did to him, as well. The deep throbbing of the Harley beneath her felt strong and powerful, and she had a sudden crazy urge to just keep going forever.

He slowed only when he turned onto an unpaved forest service road, rutted from wear over the years. As they slowed, she began to feel a little worn-out. Evergreens lined the road like soldiers who would stand sentinel all winter. There were few deciduous trees back here to add color, and no clearings to add sunlight. The forest began to seem dark and mysterious.

Finally, he stopped and turned off the ignition. She waited, wondering what he intended, then he pulled his helmet off and slung it over his handlebars.

"Let's take a break," he suggested.

She let go of him reluctantly and accepted his help dismounting. Her legs felt a bit shaky, but she didn't know if that was from the bike's vibration or the ebbing of the adrenaline.

"Wow," she said, and sank down on the ground, leaning back against a tree trunk.

"Sorry. Did I scare you?"

She looked up at him where he still stood beside the bike. "Hell no. That was fun."

He dropped to sit cross-legged beside her. "I think better when I'm moving."

"Apparently it has to be fast."

"It's better that way."

"I'm not complaining." She leaned her head back and closed her eyes, soaking up the scents and sounds of the autumn woods. If any animals were about, the bike had most likely scared them to a safer distance. The pine smelled so clean, and balanced the mulch smell of the decaying vegetation on the forest floor.

"So," she asked finally, "what did you think about?"

"Anything I might have done that would make me easy to identify. Anything that might link who I was then to who I am now. Nobody's perfect. I can't remember everything I said or did during those years. I might well have said a thing or two that eventually struck someone as significant."

She nodded, deciding for once to hold back her questions and let him talk about whatever he pleased. When she heard him sigh, she opened her eyes and while she had seen pain reflected there before, never had she seen him look so anguished.

"You forget who you are," he said slowly. "You become one of them. It's not just pretending, it's being. Thinking like them, acting like them, until only the slenderest thread ties you back to who you really are and why you're there. It gets into your skin, your pores and the deepest places in your brain. Sometimes you can even forget for a while that you're not one of them. And then you roll it up and walk away and you discover it's still with you, the stench and filth of being one of them."

She honestly didn't know what to say. She couldn't begin to imagine having to become and then live as the antithesis to everything you believed in, not even for a good cause. Her chest tightened as she realized how deeply scarred he must be.

"Anyway." He seemed to shake himself. "This isn't the time. We've got more important fish to fry right now. At least I do. I need to teach you self-defense, because if they find me here, they might connect you with me somehow."

Her heart skipped a beat and seemed to lodge somewhere in her throat. After seeing how disturbed he was because he'd had to become one of those people who were now chasing him, she was feeling a whole lot less cavalier about the potential danger to herself. "How dangerous are they?" she asked.

"They're fanatics, Liza. Full of zeal and self-certainty. Why would they hesitate to kill you if they were prepared to bomb—" He broke off sharply. "They studied interrogation techniques, too. And I don't mean the kind police use."

"Torture?" she whispered.

"I saw one of their victims." His gaze drifted away, seeming to see far beyond the woods. "Anything to further the cause. All of it justified by their belief in the intrinsic evil of our government, and frankly, of most of our citizens. They knew the truth, you see. And making it even worse, their leader managed to make them believe they were chosen."

She swallowed, absorbing it. "Chosen, huh? That's dangerous."

"You bet. We don't usually go to these lengths unless someone is really dangerous. Most militias and militant groups can be dismissed, or just watched from a distance. Ones like this give us nightmares."

She didn't need him to draw her a map. Part of her obsession as a reporter had been trying to understand why people did the things they did, believed the things they believed. She'd learned a lot about the malleability of the human mind.

He surprised her by reaching out to capture a lock of her hair and trail it gently through his fingers. The caress, so light, nevertheless caused a trickle of desire. Damn, she responded so quickly to him. Maybe she ought to be frightened by him. Maybe she was.

"You and I," he said, surprising her yet again, "are a lot alike."

"How so?"

"We've looked at the ugly side of human nature too much. Do you ever wish you could just be normal?"

"Oblivious, you mean?"

That caused him to give a crack of laughter. "Not exactly."

She sighed, wishing he would touch her again because it felt so good, like a bulwark against the ugliness they were skirting around. "It skewed me," she said finally. "I know it did. I have memories people shouldn't have. But I know that's not unique. I was out there with those firefighters and cops and EMTs. They have to live with it, too."

He twisted, stretching out beside her, propping himself on one elbow. He lifted a handful of dead pine needles and let them trail off his hand like sand.

"Undercover operatives have a high incidence of substance abuse, divorce, emotional problems. I avoided the first two. And I'm not naive enough to think I can ever go back to seeing the world the way I did when I was a kid. But I'd like to see the better side of it from here on out."

"I can understand that."

"Can you?" His blue eyes pierced her. "I get the feeling you really miss being a reporter."

"It became part of me. And it didn't give me an identity crisis like your job gave you. I guess I'm an adrenaline junkie."

"I think we both are. In my case, I know I'm ready to give it up."

She lifted a brow. "Really? You expect me to believe that after the ride we just took?"

He laughed and grabbed her, turning her until she lay beside him. Then he threw his leg over hers, captured her face between his hands, and kissed her hard.

When he lifted his head he was smiling again and she was trying to catch her breath.

"I wish," he said, "that this was just simple boy meets girl. I want to get to know you. I want us to have all the time in the world to just discover our feelings and see where they lead."

"But?"

"But. You know what's got me worried. So it's not simple."

"No."

"What's more, it's been a long time since I had a relationship that simple. I probably don't even remember how." He rolled onto his back and stared up into the tree boughs above.

She looked at him, studying his profile, trying to think of things to say. To do. Anything to find some kind of magic to dispel his concerns. Of course she couldn't think of anything. Life had taught her to be a hardheaded realist.

But with Max, she found a longing to be less realistic.

She guessed that was what he meant when he said he wished it could just be simple. Tentatively she reached out and laid her hand on his chest. To her great pleasure and relief, he covered it with his own.

"Life is never simple," she said finally. "Not any of it."

"No." He gave her hand a gentle squeeze, but continued to stare upward. She guessed he was running things through in his mind again, so she fell silent.

It was enough for now, she supposed, just to be here with him. Despite the fragrance of pine, she could smell him still, the delicious odors she was rapidly coming to associate with him. The leather jacket he wore and faint, musky scents of man.

She throbbed deep inside as she inhaled him along with the woodsy smells and wondered vaguely why she'd never before noticed that someone's scent could turn her on.

A bird called from somewhere nearby, telling her that whatever animals they'd scared away were beginning to return. Like her, she thought suddenly, and almost snatched her hand back from his chest. What was it about him that kept destroying her carefully built protective walls?

For God's sake, he'd described himself as a consummate liar, as a man who didn't know who he was, as a guy who'd participated in terrible things whatever the reason, and she knew sure as she was sitting here that he was going to hit the road as soon as these guys were caught and he no longer needed to hide.

Cripes, Liza, she scolded herself. *You know better.* Max McKenny or Kenneth Maxwell, whichever, was going to shake the local dust from his heels as soon as he could. Not even in her wildest imaginings could she envision a man like him being content in Conard County. They didn't have any conspirators, and local law enforcement helped people more than it dealt with criminals. The boredom would kill him.

With that thought, she did pull her hand back. No deeper. No further. Consider it a small, temporary fling, something to enjoy and then forget. Invest nothing of importance.

Good rules, hard to follow. She felt her jaw tighten with determination, though, even as she squeezed her eyes shut as if she could banish the sense of impending loss.

Then he whispered, "Wolves are shy, right?"

Her eyes snapped open. She saw he was looking to the side and she tried to see what he was looking at. "Do you see one?" she whispered back.

"In the bushes to my right. He's in the foliage, but he's watching. Shh."

Moving very slowly, she lifted her head a bit and looked.

It was hard at first, but then the wolf moved just a little and she saw it through the undergrowth. First two golden eyes, then the outline of a canine head and shoulders.

"Oh," she breathed.

It had a beautiful mask, a white snout and then a black arch above the eyebrows that seemed to cover the ears. After half a minute or so, it disappeared into the trees.

She held perfectly still, hoping it would return, but it didn't. And then in the distance, she heard a howl arise. Soon it was joined by another.

Max sat up. "Is that a warning?"

"I think it's an announcement of territory. We must be trespassing. They don't bother humans, though."

"This is incredible," he said, listening to the growing number of howls. "It sends chills down my spine. Fantastic!"

"They have beautiful voices, don't they?" The magic she had wanted had arrived. She sat up, too, and listened as the howls gradually faded into the distance and stopped.

"I guess we drove them off," Max remarked. "That's a pity."

"They'll be back."

"Do you know a lot about wolves?"

"Not much. Dexter told me most of what I know. They're good for the ecology, and they're shy around people. Oh, and they howl not only to locate each other but to let invaders know they own a territory. And there you have it, all of my encyclopedic knowledge."

He smiled. "That's adequate. If I decide I want to know more, I know where there's a decent library."

But then his smile faded. "I shouldn't be hanging around with you."

Her heart plummeted. Here it came, just a little sooner than expected. Why should he be the first man not to reject her? "Why not?"

"Because I could be endangering you."

"I thought I already did that to myself by checking your background."

"Maybe." He looked away.

"Don't I have anything to say about it?"

"Do you want to have something to say about it?"

She didn't have to think it over for long. She rose to her knees, turning so that she faced him directly. He looked at her. "Yes, actually, I do."

His expression never changed. "So say it."

Well, that was where things started to get complicated. She didn't know exactly what she felt other than sexual attraction. So finally she just blurted, "I have a right to make a decision. And I'm getting awfully tired of not being able to make them for myself. Don't do that to me, Max. Don't be like all the rest. I'm a grown woman. I choose my own risks."

He didn't speak, just continued to regard her steadily from those icy blue eyes. Now she felt like a fool, but that only made her angrier and more determined. She was sick of feeling like a fool.

"If I'm in danger—and that's still an unanswered question—you aren't responsible. I am. And it's a lousy reason to run anyway. Didn't you say earlier today you felt a duty to protect me?"

"I did."

"Well, I got news for you. I don't want you to hang around to protect me. I want you to hang around because you like me. So unless you want to tell me straight to my face that you don't like me—" She broke off and regarded him suspiciously. "Do you like me?" It was the most dangerous question she could ask, and her heart pounded uncomfortably. But as usual, she had to know. Her personal curse.

"Like you?" He looked astonished.

"Like me," she repeated. "Or do you just intend to get on that bike of yours and disappear from town before sundown?"

"It had crossed my mind."

"I knew it." She dropped back down to a sitting position and wrapped her arms around her upraised knees. "You must really think I'm an idiot."

"Oh, for the love of Mike..."

"No, seriously. Why else wouldn't you do me the courtesy of thinking I can make my own decisions? That I'm capable of deciding which risks I want to run. Do you honestly think I haven't had to make that decision for myself before? Well, I have, and I'm still here."

"Stop, Liza."

"Why should I stop? It's true."

A combination of pain and anger swamped her, as if they had been accumulating for years. She tried to tell herself she was overreacting, that he was right. Of course he was. Did it matter if it ended today or in a week? Because it was going to end. But her heart was hurting.

"I could leave to protect you," he said slowly. "Or I can stay to protect you. I honestly don't know which way would make you safest."

"But what do you want?" she demanded, and hated herself for revealing her own vulnerability.

"I don't know," he said bluntly. "How could I when I don't even know who I am anymore? But you turn me on like nobody ever has, and as much as you irritated me with your poking around in my past, I still like you. Trust me, I'm not in the habit of sharing my Harley with just anyone."

The way he said it penetrated her hurt, fear and anger, and a pained little giggle escaped her. "Is that what you call it?"

"Madam, you have not yet ridden that particular bike," he reminded her gravely.

"No?" Maybe not fully, but she'd certainly given it a test drive.

"Not completely." He caught her chin and looked deeply into her eyes. "So you want to stick this out with me?"

"Yes."

"Okay, until this is over, you decide whether I stay or go, I promise."

Her heart lifted and her anger began to recede. "That's fair."

But then he grew solemn again. "Liza, you have to promise me."

"What?"

"That you'll do what I say. That you'll take this threat seriously until I'm sure we're both safe. And that you'll work hard at the things I'm going to teach you."

"I always wanted to be a mini agent."

"Liza," he said almost sternly.

"I promise."

"Good."

He released her chin. She watched as he pulled out his cell phone.

"Hell, no signal. We have to go back before somebody hits the panic button. I've been out of reach too long."

"Is that your electronic leash?"

"You bet."

He helped her up, brushing pine needles from her clothing and hair with gentle hands. Then he gave himself a quick once-over.

"Time to give the wolves their territory back," he said grimly as he helped her onto the bike. "And time to get back to reality."

A lot of thoughts roared through Max's mind as he drove them back to town. The din was loud and furious like the sound of his bike.

He might have just made a huge mistake. Ames had suggested he just clear out before any more connections were made. While he was still in the clear. They could plant an article in the local paper about his leaving, in case he was traced this far.

But he didn't want to leave Liza. Even though he'd thought about it, something in her expression when he'd mentioned it had torn at him. He was playing with fire and he knew it, but he couldn't bring himself to wound her.

He told himself she'd find plenty of reasons to want to dump him before long. Parts of him still resembled the person he'd had to be over the past years, and he never knew when that person might show up.

He was also an emotional basket case in some ways, whining about who the hell he was. He'd better get over himself quickly, or he could wind up becoming one of those guys with an alcohol problem.

Let it lie, he told himself. Just let it lie. As long as someone didn't manage to take him out, he had years to sort out the mess in his head. And if someone did take him out, none of it would matter.

He wasn't afraid of dying. If he'd feared that, he never would have gone undercover. Every single moment he'd been living on the knife-edge of discovery, where just one slip could have left him dead. No, his nightmares didn't have to do with that.

But he had another nightmare now: that something might happen to Liza. On the one hand, Ames's advice made sense: cut out now before it was too late. On the other, he couldn't be positive that it wasn't too late. How the hell could anyone be certain that Liza's poking around had gone unnoticed, or that they hadn't linked it to him?

Damn, life got complicated when you lived it as different people. Sometimes keeping his own thoughts straight took effort.

Tearing down the mountain roads, he scarcely noticed the gorgeous day around him. This was a job, he reminded himself. Just like any of his other tasks. He had to protect himself as a witness, and he had to protect Liza as an innocent bystander.

For now he couldn't afford to think of anything else. He had to focus and let everything else slide. Until he was sure Liza hadn't been linked to him, he couldn't leave. If it turned out the link had been made, then he was going to scoop her up, take her away and put her in his private version of the WITSEC program. In fact, if those links were made, he might not even tell Ames where he was going.

It's not as if he didn't have plenty of money. Going undercover had meant he'd had to work a job and live on his earnings. That was a lot of ATF salary banked.

So he could clear them both out of here if necessary and go so deep even Ames couldn't find him.

Why did he keep thinking that? The thought caught him up short and almost made him hesitate on a sharp turn.

Did he not trust Ames? But that was ridiculous. If Ames wanted to out him for some reason, he could have done so any time in the past five years.

No, something else was bothering him.

How had the militants figured out who he really was? He remembered Jody, their hacker, and while the guy was good, was he that good? Liza had tracked him back from this end, but only as far as Stetson. She wouldn't have gotten any further; he was sure of that.

But tracking him from the militant end should have

been even harder. That was the path they'd buried the deepest and for a long time now.

Something didn't feel right.

And he'd learned never to ignore that instinct.

Far away, a name was spoken in a moment of seeming sexual conquest. That name was squirreled away and carried back to a dingy room in an abandoned building. Jody set to work on his computer, tracing the name. Occasionally he muttered a curse, and something about going back to the beginning.

The others waited impatiently. So much time had already lapsed that their leaders had begun to make threats against them from within the walls of the federal detention facility. Threats they all knew could be carried out, because not all of their pawns had been rounded up.

"Relax," Jody said.

"Relax?" The woman almost growled the word. "You know how many pawns we still have out there. Every single one of them could be turned into an unquestioning missile against us. That's what we turned them into, remember."

"And they wouldn't have any trouble finding us, not like we've had finding Max," one of the other guys pointed out.

Almost simultaneously, three of them lit cigarettes, a nervous response.

"Just shut up," Jody said. "You're slowing me down."

Three hours later the connection was made.

"If we drive straight through," Rose said, "we can get there in a few days."

She looked around and saw five answering nods.

They could take turns at the wheel, and they wouldn't have to stop for anything except gas and food.

She smiled, stripped and climbed back into her cammies.

Chapter 8

As they returned to town, Max pulled up at the La-Z-Rest. "What's going on?" Liza asked as he turned off his bike.

"I just want to grab my stuff." He paused, squeezed her shoulder. "I'll just be a second. Trust me, you don't want to come inside unless you're interested in water-stain maps that look like Texas."

So she sat on the bike waiting, trying not to move in case the kickstand should give way. He was right; he returned in less than a minute with a pack he stuffed into one of the panniers.

"What's that?" she asked as he remounted. His answer was drowned as he turned over the ignition and the bike roared to life again.

Well, she supposed she would find out soon enough.

He drove around the block where her apartment was

a couple of times before parking in a visitor slot one building over.

More secret agent stuff she supposed as he helped her dismount. At her apartment, he insisted on entering first and checking everything out before he told her to come in.

"Isn't this a little extreme?" she asked once they were locked inside.

"Probably. But I've got a feeling and I never ignore a feeling."

"A feeling about what?"

"That something isn't right."

She didn't immediately ask, maybe because feelings could be hard to explain, and she was familiar with that particular one. She'd felt it often enough as a reporter when she had absolutely nothing to point at to explain it.

The afternoon sun had started to pour through the west windows, making the apartment feel warm and a little stuffy, especially after they'd been outside for so long.

She opened some windows a few inches and was glad to feel a cool breeze begin to move through the rooms.

She started fresh coffee, brought out some rolls and cold cuts and put them on the table with condiments. Then she opened her book bag to get to work on the week's lessons.

Max had said not a word, but he was prowling again.

"Help yourself," she said, pointing to the table.

"Thanks."

She waited, but he made no move toward the table. Finally the words burst from her: "What in the world has you so jumpy?"

He threw up a hand. "I'm not sure. Well, maybe a little."

"So tell me before I go nuts."

He sighed and ran his fingers impatiently through his hair, combing it back from his forehead where his helmet had plastered it. "It's just a feeling, Liza. Just a feeling. I still can't figure out how they found out who I was so fast. The links between my cover job and ATF were buried so deep they probably reached the topsoil of China."

The humor didn't work. "You said they had a great hacker."

"There's great and then there's great." He finally sat in a chair at the table. "Maybe I'm getting hyped for no reason. But believe me, it was easier for you to figure out who I was than it should have been for them."

"Maybe they've been at it longer."

"Maybe. But all the walls were built to prevent them from tracking out to me. Few were built to prevent you from tracking back to me. Regardless, everything should end at ATF. That should be the impenetrable wall."

She nodded and pulled out her desk chair to sit. "I can see that."

"Anyway, it's like with a crime. If you know who did it, it's a whole lot easier to follow the trail back to the victim than it is to follow the trail from the victim when you don't have any suspects. That's why cops are so eager to build a list of suspects."

"Right." Then a thought struck her. "In your case, the easiest place to follow a trail from would be right in the middle."

"At ATF," he agreed.

"You think your handler...?"

He shook his head. "If he'd wanted to out me, he could have done it anytime over the past five years. Easily. And it would have all been laid to my door. No, it's not Ames. And maybe it's nobody."

"But you're still wondering."

"Yeah."

Well, that was a pretty picture, she thought. Now he was wondering if he'd been betrayed. As she knew all too well, people were untrustworthy with secrets. Even agents.

"What do we do?" she asked.

"Wait. Act like everything's normal."

"Except stay on high alert."

"Yeah."

"Eat," she said after a pause, because there was nothing else to say. "Those rolls will go stale sitting out."

He turned toward the table and reached for a roll. For her part she felt no appetite at the moment. Instead she powered up her computer, checked her email and then set to work on the slide presentation she planned for this week. More work on ledes, of course, and the basics of a news story.

She forced her attention on her job because it didn't seem like there was anything else she could do right now.

Not a damn thing.

At some point he set a sandwich at her elbow. She thanked him, keeping her attention on her lecture even though her mind wanted to head in any other direction. Work first. It was an old reminder and it saved her now. You couldn't work on a newspaper under daily deadlines if you couldn't corral your thoughts.

She heard him moving things around behind her and

looked just long enough to see he had cleared up lunch and was now opening a laptop and spreading some papers around. Probably preparing for his classes, too.

The afternoon passed quietly. She closed the windows when the temperature started to drop after sundown, and returned to her desk, determined to get the whole week of classes ready. Who knew what might happen to distract her later?

She kept at it doggedly until his phone rang. She wished she were a cool enough customer to ignore it, but she wasn't. Her heart skittered a bit and she swiveled her chair around to look at him.

Max stared at his phone as if something was wrong.

"Max?"

He held up a finger, then pressed a button and held the thing to his ear. "Yeah?"

The conversation on his end was monosyllabic, indecipherable. She sat and waited, clenching her hands on her lap.

He hung up swiftly and swore.

"What?" she asked.

"Ames. Calling me from his personal landline."

"Is that bad?"

"Maybe. He told me to get a new phone immediately and call him back with the number."

She blinked. "He thinks you can be traced by a cell phone?"

"I don't know," he said impatiently. "Is there anywhere around here to get a new phone?"

"Not right now. We roll up the streets at night, especially on Sunday. You can get one in the morning."

"Hell." He passed his hand over his face.

"Max? Talk to me, please. What's going on?"

"I think something gave him the same feeling I got.

I don't think he has anything to hang it on or he would have told me, but calling me from his home phone, and telling me to ditch this one…" He shook his head.

"It doesn't sound good," she agreed. Her adrenaline was up again, making her feel a bit edgy. She rose from her desk and did something she seldom worried about on the second story: she drew all the curtains and blinds.

When she came back from the bedroom, she found Max disassembling his phone, pulling out the battery and the chip. He crushed the chip between his fingers then looked at her.

"Got something I can burn this in?"

She brought him a plate and a lighter she kept handy for her stove's pilot light. He held the flame to the crushed chip and they watched it burn.

That, more than anything that had so far happened, told Liza she was entering a new world with new rules.

"Will that do it?" she asked.

"It should. It's not a smartphone. I should probably still smash it, though."

"I'll get you a hammer." She returned from her hall closet with one in hand and they went out onto her small balcony so he could smash it on the concrete. "You know," she said, as he swept up the pieces, "this is scaring me."

He eyed her with mild amusement. "Finally?"

"I don't usually scare easily. And so far it's been all speculation."

"And smashing the phone changes that how?"

"Simple. You don't smash a perfectly good phone based on speculation."

Her words arrested him for a moment. He scanned

the area behind her building, now in dusk, then said, "Let's go inside."

He chose to sit at her small dining table, as if to put space between them. She got cups of coffee for them both and then they sat facing one another.

"Okay," she said, "I want it all. Your handler must have said something."

"Not really. He told me to pack up and move on. I refused. Then he told me to smash my phone and get a new one."

"That speaks volumes to me. Who the hell could trace you by your phone except the phone company or someone from the government? I'm good at searching for stuff, Max, and I can sure as hell tell you I couldn't trace your phone for love or money. You need a warrant for that."

"I know."

"So what's going on?"

"I don't know." He sighed almost sharply. "Look, he told me all I need to know. He's worried. He's uneasy enough to tell me to change phones, uneasy enough to call me from his personal landline, from home. If he knew anything he'd tell me."

"But instead he told you just enough to put you on high alert."

"That's all I need, and he knows it."

"Damn." She looked down at her mug and started turning it between her hands. "Maybe you should leave, Max. Just get on your bike and clear out tonight. I can tell the school tomorrow that you had a family emergency. Someone can surely find a substitute to cover your classes fast enough."

"I'm not going to leave unless I have a reason to.

Nothing Ames said makes me think I've been found, only that he's worried it could happen."

"And he's worried that it's one of your colleagues."

"He didn't say that."

"He didn't have to say that! If he's worried about a phone tracer, it would have to come from somewhere inside some agency that knows about you. I know you're not an idiot, and I'd appreciate it if you wouldn't treat me like one."

He stared at her steadily. "I know you're not an idiot. But I'm not leaving you here until I'm sure you're safe."

"I'm plenty safe. Once you're gone, nobody's going to care about me. And for Pete's sake, they don't even know you're here! Didn't you say that? They haven't made this connection yet. So for now we're both safe."

"Then why are you suggesting I hit the road?"

"Because I'm worried about you!"

"Then do me the courtesy to accept that I'm worried about you, too."

They were glaring at each other like a couple of elk ready to butt heads, Liza realized. The only thing they weren't doing was pawing the ground.

Tension, she thought. The tension had suddenly reached a fever pitch. But why? Nothing had really changed. Nothing had really happened. Yet the tension was in the air like electricity before a storm.

What was going on?

And then she met Max's eyes, and she knew.

He stood up abruptly. The chair fell over behind him but he ignored it. He rounded the table in a flash and lifted her right out of her chair. She gasped as she realized he was carrying her toward her bedroom.

"Say no now, Liza," he said tautly. "It's your last chance."

She realized then what had been going on. All day long they had been dancing around this, talking about everything else, however pointlessly, and all the while the growing tension had next to nothing to do with any possible threat and everything to do with the hunger that had been zapping between them.

She didn't say no. She couldn't.

It had been a long time since Max had had an opportunity to practice any real finesse with a woman. If he'd ever known how, he was fairly certain he'd forgotten.

All day long he'd been leashing himself, not wanting to give in to the hunger that her every sigh seemed to stoke. He wanted her, wanted her more than he could remember wanting anyone since he'd been sixteen and his hormones had raged enough that he'd wanted sex constantly.

But he was much older and more experienced now. Hormones had been something he'd long since learned to control.

Until Liza. He cussed himself for being ten kinds of idiot right before he knocked that chair over and scooped her up.

Where had his control gone? Damned if he cared. Whatever had been going on inside him, all the mess he felt from once again changing identities, reflections about his life and finding himself, had exploded into a need to make a very real human connection, something he hadn't allowed himself in years because it was too dangerous.

He couldn't care about the people he was investigating. It would have affected his performance, and it didn't matter that some of them seemed like very nice, albeit seriously misguided people. He couldn't allow himself to care about people who weren't involved because that could draw them into danger. Or he'd hurt them with his long, unexplained absences.

So he'd been living a very emotionally isolated existence, caring only about job and duty, with Ames as his only contact with the outside world.

He was starved for something real. Something that wasn't a lie. For something that wasn't layered over with all the crap involved in being undercover.

He could no more resist the lure than he could have given himself over to the enemy.

He had one last sane thought: he hoped he wasn't going to hurt Liza. Then thought vanished before a flood of need.

When he lifted her into his arms, he knew that nothing had ever felt so right. And for now, he didn't need to think, just feel—it had been so long since he had enjoyed that luxury.

As he carried her to her bedroom, he offered her a chance to say no because conscience demanded it. And when all she did was turn her face into his shoulder, relief weakened him almost as much as hunger strengthened him.

Her bedroom was dark now, but he felt her stir against him as he set her on her feet and heard a switch click. Light poured from a small bedside lamp to guide him. His heart thudded with eagerness, and the swelling in his groin ached and throbbed in time with it.

Nothing could happen fast enough. Nothing. Finesse? Maybe later.

It was all he could do not to literally rip the clothes from her body. He fumbled impatiently at buttons and thrilled when he felt her small fingers helping him.

Then, as he tossed her shirt aside, she reached for the

hem of his T-shirt and started to pull it up. Impatiently he reached for it himself, yanking it over his head. The air felt cool on his heated skin, like a sinuous caress.

For an instant he thought she had changed her mind, and a chill started to drench him. But she only stepped back a few inches before reaching for the clasp of her bra.

Holding his breath, he watched as she released it and shrugged the white wisp of material away. Her breasts fell free, beautiful breasts with puckered pink nipples.

Arrested, he stared, his body growing harder and heavier still until he was filled with an ache unlike any he could remember.

"Touch me," she whispered.

He needed no further invitation. He gave himself over to finding what he had needed for so long.

Reaching out he cupped both her breasts, loving the way they filled his hands, loving the way her nipples felt hard against his palms, loving the way she gasped and tilted her head back, asking for more.

He was in no mood to deny her. In fact, he doubted that anything could have stopped him then. He leaned forward, drawing one nipple into his mouth, sucking it strongly, listening to the soft moan that escaped her.

Her response fueled him to new heights. While he sucked on her, he fumbled with her jeans and managed finally to unsnap them and push them down. Then he felt her do the same to him, allowing him to spring free of confinement.

When her hand closed around his staff, he thought he would die from the pleasure.

Nor could he wait any longer. He swept her up and laid her on the bed, pulling away the last of her clothing. Somehow he managed to ditch his own, including the damn boots he always wore, and he only spared a moment to take in the beauty spread before him on a colorful quilt.

She was perfect. From her cat-green eyes, to her nicely rounded breasts, from her narrow waist to her smooth stomach, from the thick thatch of dark hair at the top of her thighs to her tiny ankles, he wouldn't have changed a thing.

Then she lifted her arms and he fell on her, taking just enough care to ensure he didn't hurt her.

There'll be time later, some voice whispered. Time for all the rest of it.

Right now he was driven by one paramount need. He paused just long enough to open a condom she had pulled out of her bedside drawer, just long enough to shudder with delight as she rolled it onto him.

Just long enough for her to open her legs and lift him.

Then he plunged home, filling her with himself, and filling himself with answers to needs long unmet.

With each movement he drove himself deeper, as if he wanted to get entirely inside her. With each thrust he heard a moan escape her, felt her nails dig into his shoulders, encouraging him, begging him.

Then she locked her legs around him as if she could surround all of him.

That did it. He drove hard, fast, taking the last few steps to the precipice. He felt her clench her muscles around him, felt the spasms of her climax and heard her cry of completion.

When he at last jetted into her, it was as if he had emptied his troubled soul.

Liza didn't want to ever move again. Every single part of her felt utterly drained, utterly soft, utterly satisfied. The weight of Max on top of her was good, welcome, right.

The cool air delighted her where it touched her hot damp skin. His skin against hers was an amazingly good intimacy. And she loved the way his muscled back rippled beneath her hands. She loved the whisper of his heavy breathing in her ear, loved having his head right beside her own.

"I'm sorry," he muttered.

Fear entered her heart. Did he regret this? "For what?"

"Being so rough and impatient."

She smiled even though he couldn't see it, relieved. "I liked it. Couldn't you tell?"

"Sort of."

She made a sound of protest as he started to roll away, but he kept going. He rose and went to the bathroom, and she waited impatiently, wondering what was next.

He returned quickly, though, and lay beside her, running his hand gently along her side, trailing his gaze over her from head to toe.

"You are beautiful," he said.

She flushed. "So are you."

And he was. Now that she had time to really look at him, she was sure she'd never seen a more perfect specimen of manhood. Perfectly proportioned, muscled but not too much. And his skin…she couldn't resist reaching out to lay her hand on his chest and feel him again.

He covered her hand with his at once, and smiled into her eyes. "Are you warm enough?"

"I'm feeling perfect."

His smile widened. "You most certainly are perfect. Thank you." He dropped a kiss on her lips.

"Don't thank me. I enjoyed every minute." With her fingertips, she traced a circle on his chest. "I think this was building all day like a thunderstorm. The air was sizzling with it." She met his gaze. "I've never had that happen before."

"Me, either."

It was a wonderful luxury, she thought, to be lying naked with him like this, naked and comfortable. To possess the freedom to reach out and touch him however she wanted.

He closed his eyes, smiling, as if he were drinking in the moment. Then his blue eyes snapped open. "Tell me about you."

"What about me? I think you know most of the essentials."

"I know some facts. I don't know the important stuff. Like, do you want to keep teaching? Or do you have other plans? What are the hopes and dreams that make up Liza Enders?"

"You don't ask the easy questions, do you."

"Nope. But I get the feeling from things you said that you aren't happy about your career change."

"Ah." She sighed, part of her sorry that he wanted to visit difficult places, and part of her touched that he even cared. Even if this was a fling for him, he wasn't treating it as one.

"You don't have to tell me."

"No. I was just enjoying the escape to paradise. Reality isn't nearly as good."

"What we just shared is reality."

His eyes were serious, almost stern.

"I know," she admitted, experiencing a little shiver of pleasure that he wasn't trying to dismiss or move away from their lovemaking. "It's just that...oh, hell. I was miserable when I was laid off. Absolutely crushed. I mean, it wasn't like I couldn't see it coming. We were having huge layoffs every quarter. Sooner or later I figured it would reach me. But I hoped it wouldn't."

"You loved your job."

"More than that. It was my identity. Everything else took second place to Liza Enders, staff reporter. Then one day that wasn't me anymore."

"I can identify with that."

"Probably more than many," she agreed. "Of course, I didn't give up, but nobody's hiring. So finally I realized I needed to do something else. Part of that was coming home. I could have taught at a few other places, but I wanted to come back here. Maybe because I thought I could find the potential mes that had existed before I chose my path in life."

"Makes sense."

"Maybe. Or maybe it was a childish response, to run home. But I learned what everyone learns—you can't go home. The town has changed some, of course, but I've changed more. I'm not going to get in touch with eighteen-year-old Liza again. She's gone."

He nodded, and smoothed his palm along her side. "I don't think any of us can do that. And maybe we shouldn't anyway. Experience makes us who we are."

"Exactly."

"So you're still not sure about teaching?"

She shook her head, then shivered a little as he ran his palm over her again. "I started for the summer semester, one class. It was okay. So far I'm enjoying this semester. But I still haven't made a full shift from reporter to instructor. I feel a bit like I'm in a holding pattern, but maybe that's just temporary."

"Are you still looking for jobs in news?"

She bit her lip, then shook her head again. "No. I realized something else."

"What's that?"

"If I never again have to see a shattered body of a sixteen-year-old on the highway, I'll be glad."

He froze for a second, then gathered her close in a tight hug. "I'm sorry," he murmured. "I'm sorry. I can imagine how awful that is."

Something in his tone, however, told her that he wasn't imagining, but remembering something similar. She forced herself to move on, because neither of them needed to remember. "But that's why most newspapers have such good mental health insurance. I think I told you, though, the cops, the firemen, the EMTs, they all have to deal with it, too."

"So you got there before it was all cleaned up?"

"Of course. We had scanners and listened to them all the time. When the call came in for cops and everybody else, I hopped in my car and went. It was my job. Of course, none of what I saw made it into the story. No, I was just supposed to be there to gather information, and then the next day I had to interview families. At least I learned not to ask stupid questions, like how do you feel about losing your son?"

"No? What did you ask?"

"How they wanted their kid, or husband or whoever to be remembered."

His hand began stroking her back. "That was a good question."

"It made me feel less like a vulture." She fell silent for a little while, enjoying the way he stroked her back comfortingly, fighting her way out of a place she tried never to go.

"Anyway," she said presently, "that's water over the

dam, as they say. Done. Finished. Locked away for good. It's only since I got here, though, that I realized I never wanted to go back to that. Oh, there are subjects I could cover for the news happily, but with short staffing these days, too many reporters are being asked to fill in on the cop beat. I can't do that anymore."

"But you still like adrenaline."

A little laugh escaped her. "You noticed."

"Yup. And that's why I asked. There's not much adrenaline in teaching."

"Not until I met you."

He laughed, then surprised her by giving her a playful swat on her bottom. "I hate to break this up, but I'm starving. Although I'm not done with you yet."

She liked the sound of that. She gave him a gentle push and he rolled right off the bed, making her laugh.

"Last one in the kitchen cooks."

He beat her, barely.

Chapter 9

In the morning, after a night that involved too little sleep and much more lovemaking that left Liza feeling pleasantly sore, they took off together on his bike to go to the cell phone store before class.

It was a gorgeous morning, smelling of frosts yet to come, the light painfully clear. Overnight, the trees seemed to have grown more golden and orange, and as the sunlight struck them, they radiated their own light.

The store was downtown in an old storefront at odds with its glaringly modern sign. Impossible to miss.

As they dismounted to go inside, Liza had an idea. "Should I buy the phone? Keep your name out of it?"

He gave it a moment's thought. "It might help. Then again, it just might draw the net tighter around you."

She shook her head a little. "No good answers. Well, me buying a phone isn't going to reach anybody's radar anywhere. Of that I'm sure. So let me get it."

All he wanted was the cheapest, most disposable phone he could find. "Something I can smash if I need to."

Well, there were plenty of those available. He picked one and they bought enough minutes to cover him for at least a month. Then, once they were out on the street, he made her put his new number into her phone.

"Just don't label it Max," he said. "Use some other identifier."

She thought that was taking caution to the extreme but she followed his directions and called him Abe.

"Why Abe?"

"Because it'll be the first name when I go to my directory."

He smiled. "Good thinking."

"Are you really that worried about this?"

"When my boss tells me to wreck my cell phone, yes."

He had a point. The glow left from last night seeped away as the morning grew steadily brighter. Reality again.

"When's your first class?" he asked. "Or better yet, when would be a good time to go to the gym? I want to teach you some moves."

More reality. But it spurred her adrenaline a bit, and like the junky she was, it elevated her mood again. "I have free time after eleven. My next class isn't until three."

"Okay then. I just hope the gym isn't packed. I don't want an audience."

"Why not?"

"Because this is going to seem weird, me teaching you self-defense moves. People will talk about it."

"Then we'll just call it a class and you can show all the girls. I'm sure they'll swarm for the opportunity."

He winked. "I'll only have eyes for you."

She pushed at his arm. "Yeah, right."

He laughed. Then he punched a number into his phone. "Yeah, it's me. Let me give you the new number." He recited it quickly. "Okay. Talk to you later."

"Your handler?" she asked as he disconnected.

"Who else. Breakfast? Or do you need to get to class?"

She glanced at her watch. "I've got time for a roll and some coffee."

"If Maude will let you escape with that."

Maude frowned but didn't argue this once. Liza got her roll and coffee. Max got steak and eggs, which evidently mollified Maude enough that she even provided coffee refills without sniffing at Liza.

Gage arrived almost as soon as they were served, and he pulled up a chair to their booth. Maude didn't even ask him what he wanted. She slammed the coffee in front of him and stalked off.

"No breakfast?" Max asked.

"I always let her decide." Gage shrugged. "I take it Liza is in your confidence?"

"What makes you think that?" Liza asked.

"A black Harley parked outside the building next to yours overnight."

"Oh." Her cheeks flamed.

Gage laughed. "Forget it. No one else has any reason to make the connection, and if they do they sure won't be talking about it to strangers." He eyed Max. "We gossip like mad in town, but only with people we know."

"Okay. So what's up?"

"I've been thinking. It's not enough that I know what's going on. So I'm going to introduce you to a few people you can trust with your life."

Max arched a brow. "You know that goes against the playbook."

"Sometimes you have to. I see two choices here, and judging by where I saw a Harley last night, one of them appears to be out of the question. The other is that I get you more backup. If you get word the crap is about to hit the fan, you just gather up Liza and go."

"That's the plan."

"Wait a minute," Liza said. "I have something to say about this."

All of them fell silent as Maude stomped up to them and put a plate in front of Gage. It was loaded with ham, eggs and home fries.

"Emma's going to kill me," Gage remarked.

Maude snorted. "Not likely. That gal is too much in love with you." Then she stomped away.

Gage's eyes twinkled. "Maude's more likely to kill me with food."

"I heard that, Sheriff!" Maude called over her shoulder.

All three of them laughed, as did some of the other diners.

But as the laughter faded, Liza leaned forward. "I don't like the idea of being carted out of town."

Gage shrugged. "Deal with Max on that one. My concern here is to get you both some more cover. I have two guys in mind. I'll take you to meet them after breakfast." He looked at Liza. "You can come if you want, but you already know them. Nate Tate and Micah Parish."

"I have to get to class." She was still annoyed by the idea of having no say in whether she would stay or go if something happened, but she had to accept that now wasn't the time to argue about it. They were in a public place, and Gage had left it up to Max. So it was with Max that she was going to have a few choice words. Later.

Max was acutely aware that Liza was annoyed, but he couldn't talk sense to her right now. He barely got her to the campus on time for her class, and then he roared away toward the sheriff's office to meet these guys Gage had mentioned.

Last night had been incredible, and he'd been trying to hang on to it like some kind of talisman until Gage had appeared and reminded him that whether he liked it or not, he still had a job to do. That job involved getting himself—alive—into a courtroom at the proper time, and protecting Liza if she crossed the radar of the militants.

Being instructed to kill his cell phone had bothered him more than he wanted to tell Liza. She'd caught on to what it could mean, but she was blithely ignorant of just how much that warning from Ames meant. Ames wasn't the type to invent concerns. His imagination never ran away with him, which was why he was such a good handler. He was factual and realistic to a fault.

So if Ames was worried about a phone trace, that meant he had a damned good reason. It meant he knew something, and what he knew was enough to worry him.

And a worried Ames was enough to heighten Max's state of alert to the top of the charts.

He didn't like leaving Liza alone on campus, but

he reasoned she'd be safe in a classroom, and he intended to be back in time to meet her right after class. Ames hadn't given him any reason yet to think he'd been found, but the time for taking chances had passed. It was time to start assuming the worst.

He gave Liza a kiss as he dropped her off, then watched until she entered her building. Ten minutes later he was walking into the sheriff's office.

Velma, the dispatcher, took one look at him through a cloud of cigarette smoke and cocked her head toward the back. "He's waiting for you."

For the first time it struck him just how much he must stand out in this small town. Maybe the agency should have stashed him in a big city. Here it seemed he had an invisible sign around his neck: Outsider.

Of course, that could work to his advantage, too. He'd turned a lot of things to his advantage in his life, and he could see how this one could be useful. If any other outsiders appeared, it would probably be on the grapevine immediately.

He found Gage in his backroom office with two other men. He was a little startled. They were both big men, and both older than he had expected. One, clad in the local uniform of Western shirt and jeans, had gray hair, a permanent sunburn and was introduced as the retired sheriff, Nate Tate. The other, a mountainous man with coal-black hair and eyes, and a face that was clearly etched as Native American, wore a deputy's uniform. Micah Parish.

"Nate and Micah," Gage said, "are both former Special Ops. They're also damn good cops. I figure we need finesse here and not extra muscle, if you get me."

Max nodded, taking the measure of Nate and Micah with his eyes, and liked what he saw. Both were fit and had the centered calm of men who knew exactly what they could do.

"Thanks," he said. "I admit I'm not exactly comfortable with this. I've always gone solo."

"We won't get in your way," Nate said in a gravelly voice. "We'll just be around. Keeping an eye out. You can't stay awake round the clock, and you can't be with Liza every minute. Between the three of us, one of us will be the first to get word if strangers come to town. We always do. So think of us as an outer perimeter."

Max nodded slowly. "I can deal with that."

Nate smiled. "I thought you could. Neither Micah nor I are spring chickens anymore. We're not going to act like it. But we talk with a lot of people every day, and we hear about everything that happens in this county."

Micah nodded once. "This whole county is one big intelligence network, but you don't get to tap into it unless they know you. That's why you need us and Gage. If six guys toting rifles suddenly show up, you'd be the last one anyone would tell. We'd be the first."

"I get it." Max allowed himself to relax a bit. "And I'm grateful. But I'm so used to being alone and depending on myself and my own wits, I'm still a little uneasy about so many people knowing who I really am."

"I can understand that," Gage answered. "But ATF let me know. A courtesy, of course, but also a recognition that I'd been an undercover operative, too. They figured I might be useful to you. I'm exercising my discretion here. You need a wider intelligence net."

Max pondered for a moment. He didn't like so many people knowing who he really was, but maybe that feeling was out of place here. They were right about one thing: he certainly wasn't hooked into the local talk. Not at all. Nobody volunteered anything to him. Oh they were friendly, all right, and made him feel welcome, but he was well aware that he was still an outsider. He wasn't invited into the kinds of conversations that made him feel as if he belonged.

And while he hadn't belonged in a long time, not really, he knew what it felt like from having been accepted by extremists. He had been aware since arriving here that he was out of the information loop, but he'd been relying on Ames and, he admitted, Gage. Originally, he'd just assumed he was safe, and hadn't worried about it. He'd be leaving soon enough.

Ames's concern had changed all of that.

"Okay," he said. "Here's where I stand. Liza traced me back to ATF. I gather someone at the other end, in the militant group I helped bust, traced me to ATF from their end. No one seems sure how they did it, but last night my handler told me to destroy my cell phone."

At that the other three men stiffened. He didn't need to explain that to them. "So if they make the connection between me and here, Liza could be in danger because she was looking into me. I'm more worried about her than I am about myself. Mainly because even if I disappear they may think she knows where I am."

"Ideally," Micah said, "you should both hit the road and leave us to handle anybody who shows up."

"Liza doesn't like that idea," Gage remarked. "Someone needs to talk some sense to her."

"I'm going to try," Max answered, "but I get the feeling it's not going to work."

"She doesn't believe there's any danger?"

"I don't think that's it, but I'm going to try to get to the root of it today. She's not at all foolish, so there's something going on with her. Maybe she just doesn't want to run unless there's a real threat." He shrugged. "She has a job, after all. Disappearing could make her future difficult."

He got three nods in response.

"Okay," Nate said. "That sets our parameters for now. Can't say I like them. That leaves one little problem."

"Which is?"

"You're entirely too trackable if they get this far. You have to keep a class schedule."

Max nodded. "I figured if I got word that they were coming, I could get someone to cover class for me."

"I'll do it," Nate said. "I've taught criminology a couple of times over the past few years. In fact, you stole my job."

Max grinned. "Blame it on ATF."

"I did. They didn't care."

Everyone chuckled. But then Nate leaned toward him, his gaze steady and serious. "I've known Liza since she was born. I don't care what it takes. We're going to protect her first."

Max nodded. "I hoped you'd say that. I can take care of myself. I'm just really annoyed that she got into the middle this way."

"Annoyed?" Nate cocked a brow. "I saw where your Harley was parked last night. How's that helping?"

"I'm keeping an eye on her." But it was more than that, a whole lot more than that even if he didn't want to say so. But he saw something in Nate's gaze that told him the older man understood.

"Ditch the bike," Nate said. "At the very least, don't park it anywhere near Liza."

Cripes, there was nothing unique about the bike, but

maybe he'd underestimated how observant folks around here were. "I just bought it a month ago. It's not like I brought it with me."

"Doesn't matter. It's registered. That's enough."

Max felt like an utter fool then. He'd been thinking that it was okay since his new identity hadn't been discovered. But the minute the militants found Max McKenny, they'd know about Max McKenny's bike. "Hell," he said. "I learned some bad habits, I guess. As long as everything fits with the new identity, it's safe. Was safe. Not now, I guess."

"It's a different way of thinking," Gage agreed. "Once you accept that an identity can be penetrated, everything changes, including standard operating procedures."

Max gave that a lot of thought as he drove back to the college. Gage was right, he decided. What had worked in the past could work against him now. He needed to reverse his thinking in major ways.

Only then did he realize how habituated he had become with the rules of maintaining a false identity. That habituation might be about ready to bite him on the butt.

Damnation!

He ditched his motorcycle in the parking lot, locked his helmet away in one of the panniers and went to meet Liza as she emerged from the classroom.

She arched a brow at him. "Time for gym?"

"I want to talk to you first."

"Okay, where?"

"Anywhere we can have some privacy." He reached for her hand, trying to tell her he hadn't forgotten last night, and he was relieved when she didn't pull away.

She looked beautiful, he thought, with the midday

sunlight bringing out the red highlights in her auburn hair. The breeze tossed it around a bit, reminding him of how silky and soft it felt in his hands. Then, inevitably, he remembered how good she felt in his hands, under him and over him. His groin ached at the memory and he had to shake himself mentally. Not the time or place.

She led him to a spot he hadn't seen before. Near the edge of campus, there was a quiet grotto with an artificial waterfall, several stone benches, and an ornamental pond. A small granite stone announced it was a memorial garden donated by some ladies' organization.

She sat on one of the benches and he joined her.

"You still mad?" he asked.

"A little," she admitted. "I should have some say in this mess and what I do. I am not baggage."

"I don't think anyone meant it that way, Liza." Indeed, if he were to be honest, he didn't understand her objection. There were times when you simply didn't have choices, but had to do the best thing possible. "We all just want to keep you safe."

"I get that. But I should still be consulted."

"Should I consult you if I see a tornado coming? Or should I just pick you up and run for the nearest shelter?"

At that she glared at him. In an instant he became aware of how little he really understood about women. But maybe it had nothing to do with her being a woman. Maybe it had everything to do with the way he had been living: mission-directed in every little thing, with almost no room for what he might want himself. Doing what he had to do whether he wanted to or not.

He also realized how badly he wanted those cat-green eyes to smile at him again. "Liza, what am I not getting? Because obviously I'm not getting something."

As he watched, her glare faded and her expression grew troubled. "Is it too much to ask that someone ask me?"

"In some situations," he insisted. "But we aren't there yet, obviously, so I'll ask. If it becomes necessary, will you leave town with me?"

"No."

"No?"

"No."

She might as well have grown two heads. He stared at her, flummoxed, then demanded, "Why the hell not?"

She looked down and he followed her gaze to see that she was twisting her fingers together until her knuckles turned white.

"Liza?"

"I won't do it, Max. Last winter my entire life seemed to come to an end when I was laid off. I lost my identity, my sense of purpose, any feeling of usefulness I had. I spent months hunting for a new position at a paper, any paper, and I couldn't find one. In the end I had to give up. Do you know how much I hated that?"

"I can imagine," he admitted.

"Maybe. Maybe not. Regardless, my life and my self-image were shredded, and I had to deal with that. And then I started making a new life for myself here, teaching. I'm still recovering from the crisis, Max. Why in the hell would I want to run away and have to start all over again? Who would I be then? Liza Enders, Quitter?"

"It wouldn't be…"

"It might as well be." She jumped up from the bench

and turned to face him, throwing up a hand. "Don't you see? I've lost enough since February. I am not going to do that again."

Whoa, he thought, as he realized how many land mines he'd just stumbled onto. Not knowing what else to do, he reached out and tugged her onto his lap, holding her tightly. At first she resisted, but he hung on, and eventually she relaxed against him.

"Okay," he said huskily. "Okay." He looked down at her and saw a tear leaking from beneath one of her eyelids. It hurt her that much. "Okay," he said again as he wiped the tear. "But can I at least toss you into a nearby storm shelter when I see a tornado?"

He felt her stiffen again, but finally she curled into him. "Teach me some self-defense so I don't need a shelter."

So that's what he did. Even though he knew the danger was great, and that all the self-defense tactics in the world might not be enough.

Max met Liza after her three o'clock class and they walked back to her apartment. "Where's the bike?" she asked.

"I was advised to ditch it."

"Oh." She sighed quietly. "I just realized something."

"What?"

"That jogging only keeps a small part of me in shape."

He laughed. "Ibuprofen, here you come?"

"And a long hot shower. I don't usually indulge because we watch our water consumption around here, but I think a long one might be justified today."

A lot of muscles and joints she hadn't used in a while were starting to ache, on top of the soreness from last night that had been a pleasant reminder all day. She dragged her thoughts back from that, knowing that right now she couldn't have enjoyed trying the next chapter of the Kama Sutra. Everything was stiffening too much. "So why ditch the bike?"

"Someone pointed out to me today that I need to start thinking differently. I'm used to thinking I need to keep everything in line with my identity and that will help keep me safe."

"Makes sense."

"But this is different. If my current identity gets penetrated, anything connected to this name could lead them to me. That includes my bike. And by the way, this place is too damn nosy."

She tilted her head to look at him, wincing a little as stiff shoulder muscles objected. "Why?"

"Because I know of at least three people who weren't fooled by me parking my bike in front of the other building."

"Ah." A reluctant giggle escaped her. "No secrets around here."

"Evidently not. Except from me, anyway, and Gage is taking care of that."

"Good." She was relieved to find she could still climb the stairs to her apartment. Stiff but not a total loss, she thought with some pride. "No more news?" she asked as he followed her inside and closed the door.

"From my handler, you mean? Not a peep."

She headed straight to the kitchen and her bottle of pain reliever. "Do you think he's checking to find out if somebody outed you?"

"Maybe. Probably. He seemed pretty disturbed when he told me to destroy my old phone."

"So how many people do know?"

"Too many," he admitted grimly. He went to the cupboard to start a pot of fresh coffee. "I don't actually know. I suppose the geeks who are hiding my identity know. Probably at least one U.S. Attorney. I know we try to keep it to the minimum, but now that the case is busted open, I'm sure some additional people know. You do everything you can to keep it under wraps, but in the end someone has got to know."

She nodded, leaning back against the counter and tossing down the pills with some water. "You know, I feel like we're running on a hamster wheel. We don't know a whole lot, and our speculations are all coming to the same point—we don't really know. So I'm going to take a shower, get into my most comfortable old sweats and take a vacation from this."

"Go ahead." He smiled. "Sounds good to me, too. I'll have coffee ready when you get out."

But she didn't exactly get out of the shower for coffee. Not right away. As she was leaning on her arms against the shower wall, letting the water beat on her shoulders and back, she suddenly felt warm, wet hands touch her and start massaging. She jumped and looked back to see Max.

"Easy," he said, smiling and looking drowsy all at once.

Easy was the last thing she felt as slick soapy hands massaged her from behind. At first he just worked her shoulders, but of course it didn't stop there. Nor did she want it to stop there. His touch, because of the soap, was silken and arousing.

Around in kneading circles over her shoulders until they let go. Then down around her back and lower over her rump. When he slipped his hand into the crack between her cheeks, she thought her knees would give way.

Over and over, down her legs, then back up until she was ready to moan with need.

Up over her hips, sliding gently, teasing, avoiding the most secret place that had begun to tighten and ache. Slowly across her midriff, then at last up to her breasts.

The moan escaped her then as he kept rubbing his hands over her, never forcefully, always lightly and teasingly, but enough to make every single nerve ending tingle with need and awareness. Back and forth over her nipples until they ached for more. Then down again, slowly, promising so much and refusing to deliver.

Her eyes had narrowed to slits, but she saw him reach again for the bar of soap and lather his hands. Then they resumed their exploration, depriving her of breath, driving everything from her head except the need to be taken.

Then down finally, oh so slowly, to slip between her legs at last.

She arched as if an electric shock ran through her. He caught her with an arm beneath her breasts and drew her back against his chest. And never once did his other hand leave the most sensitive private place between her legs.

His touch was lazy, maddening, as if they had all the time in the world. But tension built in her anyway, until she felt her entire body was screaming for completion.

She shivered from head to foot, weakened by need. She felt as if she would collapse, but he didn't let her.

Again and again his hand moved, stoking the fires, lifting her ever higher.

Everything disappeared in the sudden explosion. Her legs clamped around his hand, her body arched so hard she felt she would snap, and the world behind her eyelids blossomed in brilliant sparkles of color.

She went over the edge into the best kind of oblivion.

Chapter 10

Max changed his appearance. She was startled the next week after class to come outside and barely recognize him. He had streaked his hair so that it looked almost blond and he was wearing glasses.

"What happened?" she asked.

"Cover. Come on, let's get out of here."

"No gym today?"

"Not today."

They climbed into her car together and he suggested they head out into the country toward the mountains. She definitely didn't like the way he kept looking over his shoulder.

"Max, what's going on?"

"Ames called earlier. There's been some internet activity around my current ID, and it's not traceable to you."

Shock made her heart slam, even though she'd been

half expecting this. Or maybe, at some deep level, she had never really believed it would happen. "It shouldn't be since I haven't been looking."

"Exactly."

She found a sunny turnout and pulled into it.

"Turn the car around so we can see if another car comes along."

That was when fear truly began trickling along her spine. "You think they could be here?"

"Most likely not yet. Flying would be a big risk since they're on our wanted list. But you never know."

Her hands were so tight on the steering wheel that her knuckles were white. She stared straight down the road they had just come up, dread and anger warring in her.

Finally she swore. "So you streaked your hair and got glasses? How can that be enough?"

"It'll buy me time, and that's all I need to react."

Then her stomach plunged sickeningly. "Someone gave you up."

"Maybe. Ames is certainly thinking about it."

"It had to be," she said tautly. "How else could they know who you are now?"

"I don't know. Ames has the geeks looking for security holes, but that hardly matters right now, does it?"

"Of course it matters! My God, Max, someone could be feeding them information right now about where you are, what you're teaching…" She couldn't even finish the thought. She felt almost breathless, and tried to slow her breathing down. It wouldn't obey her, because her heart was tripping like mad. "So what now?" She hated the question because she feared the answer. Truly feared it. If anything happened to Max… Another thought she couldn't complete.

"First," he said, "I'm going off the grid."

"How the hell can you do that?"

"I'm trashing my phone again, even though it's in your name. In retrospect that may have been a stupid decision, by the way. Because Ames has this number and if he gave it to anyone else, the bad guys might have it."

"Finding out who owns a cell number is next to impossible."

"Next to but not impossible."

She hated to admit he was right. "What else?"

"I don't use my credit card anymore, Nate is going to take over my classes for a while, and I need you to talk to me, Liza."

"About what?"

"Will you leave with me until they catch these guys? If they zero in on this county, plenty of people are going to be looking for them now, but I don't want you somehow caught in the middle."

Common sense told her he was right. Every emotion in her rebelled. "I told you," she said, her voice breaking. "I told you. How much am I supposed to give up? If you could promise it would be only a day or two, that would be different. But you can't. You don't know when they might show up."

"No, I don't. But if it doesn't happen in a day or two, we can set you up in protection, with a new identity."

She let go of the steering wheel and turned then to glare at him in fury. "No. Absolutely not, I don't care if Armageddon is around the corner."

"Liza…"

She held up a hand, silencing him. "No, Max. No way. I won't do it. You're talking about taking away the last shreds of who I am."

"You're not a name."

"Well, you would certainly know that, wouldn't you," she said bitterly. "But look at you, you're all mixed-up inside. I'm already mixed-up enough inside and I'm not doing one damn thing to make it worse."

With that she started the car again and headed back home. There was a limit, and he'd just pushed her limit. Enough.

Max had more than enough to think about, so he didn't say much on the ride back to her place.

If he thought leaving town would make Liza safe, he'd do so in a heartbeat, even though just thinking about it was painful. He had grown so attached to her, and he couldn't stand the thought of giving up whatever was happening between them.

But for her sake, he'd disappear.

Except that he couldn't be sure his disappearance would make her safe. If they'd located him, there were at least a dozen ways they could link her to him. He knew these people. They wouldn't hesitate to use her for bait, or even to hurt her as much as necessary if they thought it would get her to reveal where he was.

And even though Nate, Micah and Gage were on perimeter duty, he didn't put much faith in their intelligence net. Not because he doubted them, but because he knew how much time and effort the subjects had spent learning to make surreptitious entry into areas and buildings. They'd come in singly, probably at night, and position themselves. And they'd do their damnedest to make sure no one saw them.

The dirty work they'd been planning had nothing to do with being martyred or caught. No, they wanted to escape to plan another attack.

So he was seriously concerned that if they got this far no one would see them coming.

He could understand Liza, too, damn it. She was right; he'd been complaining about essentially the same thing. What if the only way they could make her safe was to strip her of the last of her identity, force her to become someone else?

He wouldn't wish that on anyone. Hell, part of that security would be tearing away even her relationship with her parents. He couldn't let it come to that.

So if that meant he had to stay and guard them both, then by God he was going to do exactly that.

After they got back, he walked her to the door of her apartment. "Lock yourself inside," he said after he checked out the place. "I'll be back shortly."

"Where are you going?"

"To get some stuff. I won't be long. Just don't let anyone in until I get back. Please. And can I use your car?"

She nodded. "Okay."

He took off fast. First to the motel where he packed all his gear in two duffels. Then downtown for some stuff from the store. While he was on his way back, he phoned Gage Dalton to make sure he'd received the message Max had left earlier.

"I got it," Gage said. "Everyone's been advised. What are you doing with Liza?"

"She won't leave. So I'm pinning myself to her side. Except when she's in class. She should be safe in class."

"Yeah, maybe. Okay, we'll keep our ears even closer to the ground and our eyes working overtime."

"Thanks."

When he reached Liza's parking lot, he looked around but saw no one. He'd have to check with management and make sure nobody new had rented in the past couple of days.

But first he headed up to Liza's place. When she opened the door to him she eyed his duffels.

"What's this?" she asked.

"My life, such as it is. You're stuck with me for the duration."

He kicked the door closed behind him and dropped his bags.

"You're protecting me?" She put her hands on her hips.

"I've been protecting you all along. The security alert level just went up, so consider me your shadow. Since we're doing this by your rules."

"Thanks," she said sharply and went to her bedroom. When he heard the door slam, he winced.

He'd been protecting her all along. The words cut Liza to the quick. That was the only reason he was staying for her, and the sex was probably just a side benefit of the job.

She fell on her bed and buried her face in her pillow as the sobs started to come. Why, oh why, had she been foolish enough to think she could trust a man this time? Because he'd opened up a little about his fears and inner struggles? That wasn't a basis for trust. It might even be a means of manipulation.

Hot tears soaked her pillow, and she bit the foam hard to stifle the sobs that racked her body violently.

Too much, she thought. God, it was all too much. She didn't want to admit she was afraid, but she was. All this time she'd only been fooling herself by thinking they didn't know that those guys would find him, or that if they did, they wouldn't even notice her.

She'd been lying to herself about everything, and she hated herself for it. She wasn't usually so stupid. Except maybe when it came to men. Her track record there wasn't exactly exemplary.

She prided herself on being smart and inquisitive. She had never been fooled as a reporter. More than one colleague had called her a human lie detector.

Except when it came to men. What the hell was wrong with her? She'd thought she'd learned her lesson the last time, but here she was again, mistaking a man's intentions.

She gulped and tried to calm herself. Okay, she was stupid about men, but that didn't mean Max was a bad man. He was worried about her safety, and he was sticking around to look after her even though it meant risking his own neck.

No, she was the problem, mistaking a man's natural sexual interest for something more.

Finally she grew too weary to cry or beat herself up any longer. She rolled over on her back and stared up at the ceiling through puffy eyes, realizing the day was fading. It was time to become the hardheaded person who had survived ten years as a reporter, the one who could look at even the most horrible things with detachment—at least until she'd done her job.

Now was no time for a breakdown or a pity party. Max's life could be on the line, and so could hers.

And then a thought struck her.

Rising, she went to wash her face in cold water, to try to hide her tears. Probably impossible, she thought when she looked in the mirror. Too bad. She draped the towel over the rack and went out to talk to Max.

She found him in her kitchen, cooking something that looked like stew. It smelled wonderful.

He looked at her. "You okay?"

"I'm fine. I think I just came to my senses, though."

He arched a brow and put down the big steel spoon he was holding. "Meaning?"

"I've been utterly selfish."

His mouth pulled to one side as if he were perplexed. "How so?"

"I've been acting like a spoiled brat. My refusing to leave means you feel you have to stay, and you could get killed. You're at even more risk than I am. So...I'll leave with you." The words were hard to speak, almost stuck in her throat in fact, but she got them out.

"No," he answered and resumed stirring the stew.

"No?"

"No." He shook his head. "I got to thinking about what you said. If we could be sure it would be only a day or two, that would be one thing. But we don't even know when they'll arrive. When I thought about what it would mean to give you a new ID—hell, Liza, you wouldn't even be able to talk to your parents anymore—I realized I couldn't do that to you. It's been hard enough for me, and I chose this. And I didn't have to give up anything permanently."

"But you could get killed."

"That's been possible in my job all along. But I'm not going to let my job destroy you. So we stay, we face them when they come and we put it to rest."

"Max..."

He turned from the stove, shaking his head. "No arguments. These guys aren't on some sort of timeline. We don't have any ticking clock to suggest when they might act."

"What do you mean?"

"I mean the trial is that far down the road. Would

they like to get their honchos out of prison? You bet. But they don't have to do that today or tomorrow or even next week. They've got a lot of time to eliminate me in order to get the charges dropped. So it's not like I can tell you you'd have to vanish for only a few days or weeks. Either we find these guys or they find us, and I can't give you the vaguest clue of when that might be."

She bit her lip and sagged into a chair at the table. "That could be a long time," she repeated almost numbly. She had figured this would come down soon, but the idea of living with this threat for months appalled her.

"How do you do it?" she asked.

"What?"

"Live with threats like this, when you don't know how long it might be, or where it might come from?"

"I've had years of practice," he answered grimly. "You get so you don't think about it…you just stay prepared for anything. I can't tell you it's going to be easy."

"And you're sure you can't just leave?" It hurt to ask it, but she couldn't ignore his safety. Just couldn't. "I mean, maybe they'll never find out about me. Maybe someone else could keep an eye on me."

"No one knows these guys as well as I do. I'll recognize them by the way they walk, unlike other agents. No, it has to be me. As for you—" he shrugged "— Ames is worried about you. That's good enough for me."

"I'll bet he's not happy with your decision to stay here."

"Ames doesn't get to be happy about my decisions. It's my job to make certain decisions, and it's not his to second-guess me. I've made up my mind. I'm not going to gut your life and I'm going to deal with this damn problem right here."

"Are they sending anyone to help you?"

"I don't need help."

"But there's six of them!"

"They won't all come. Even if they do, yes, we've got agents in place nearby, but we can't risk bringing them into a place where strangers stick out. They'll come if I call. They'll come if we get concrete information on the whereabouts of these guys. But until then, it's just you and me, babe."

Then he put down the spoon and came around to lay his hand on her shoulder. "What the hell did I say?"

"What do you mean?"

"I said something, and you stormed off. I can tell you've been crying."

No way was she going to tell him the real reason for that. She might be hurting like hell, but she still had her pride. "Nothing, really. I guess it all just kind of hit me."

He pulled a chair around and sat facing her. When he reached for her hand, she didn't have the heart to tug it away. It might all be an illusion—it probably was—but she wasn't ready to give it up yet.

"It's going to be okay," he said gently, but when she glanced at him she could see he looked troubled.

"Don't make promises," she said. "Just don't make promises. There's nothing you can promise, not my safety or yours." Or anything else, probably.

"All right," he said after a moment. "No promises. At least not now."

That night, for the first time, they shared a bed but did not touch. She lay stiffly, staring into the dark, wondering how the heck she thought it was going to save her any pain at all if she pulled back now.

It wasn't. But as raw as she felt, she still couldn't turn on her side and touch him.

She gathered he was awake, too, because she could feel the stiffness in him, most likely the result of the way she had pulled back when he reached for her.

This was going to be hell on earth, she realized. Hell on earth. Never mind what they might face if these militants arrived. Just getting through the night was going to be hard enough.

In the morning, Liza felt hung over from lack of sleep. Breakfast was almost silent as they ate oatmeal and drank coffee. Max seemed both worried and subdued, but at least he didn't try to have a conversation with her. She didn't think she could have managed it.

Trying to lift her own spirits, she put on her "dancing duds" as she thought of them. On the spur of the moment a few years ago, when she and some friends had decided to go to a country and western nightspot in Tampa for some line dancing, she'd splurged on some fancy jeans, shoes and a blouse.

Not cowboy boots, though. Those were too dang expensive and she knew in that climate she wouldn't wear them very often.

But she bought a royal-blue satin shirt, some jeans with sequins on the back pockets and some royal blue Mary Janes with small heels. She hadn't worn them since.

But when she emerged from the bedroom looking like someone who ought to be on stage singing "Your Cheatin' Heart" she got a smile from Max.

"I like that," he said. "It's sassy, especially those shoes."

"Thanks. I wore them for line dancing." And it did perk her up a bit to get the compliment.

"I love it. And if we ever get past this mess, I'll take you dancing."

"You line dance?"

"I learned in college, believe it or not. I discovered this thing about women."

"And that was?"

"They like to go dancing. And they're not happy with a guy who has two left feet."

Despite her mood, she laughed. "I'll bet you didn't have any trouble with learning."

"Nope. Somehow all the karate I took back then made it easy."

"Don't tell me you have a black belt."

So he said he wouldn't. That made her laugh again, and for a little while the day didn't look quite so dark. She told herself she would survive this emotionally. She had survived the end of longer relationships, after all.

Of course, said a voice in the back of her mind, never had she fallen so hard so fast before.

But an opposing voice answered, *Well, that means it's not real, doesn't it?*

Maybe. Whatever, there was no escape now. Not from any of it. She mentally squared her shoulders, determined to get through it all.

After all, regardless of what happened next, she had never asked Max the most important question of all: What do you intend to do when this is over?

Go back to being an agent, probably, even if he never went undercover again. And their lives would have diverged despite everything. They just weren't fated to be together, and she should have reminded herself of that from the outset.

Her own fault. She should have guarded her heart better. Much better.

In fact, when she took an objective view, she was a little appalled. She'd gone nose-diving into Max's background when she'd had no right. And she wasn't at all sure anymore that she could blame it on her curious nature. No, she'd been hoping to find something that would quell her attraction to him. Instead she'd walked into deep waters up to her neck, and possibly exposed him to danger as well as herself.

One of these days she was going to owe this man a sincere apology. But not today. Today she was still too hurt.

And it was not at all his fault.

She sighed.

"A penny for your thoughts," he said easily as they walked toward the campus.

"They're worth a dollar these days," she retorted, lame as the joke was. Looking at him, she realized he was scanning their surroundings, his eyes darting everywhere.

She was supposed to be doing that, too, she remembered. He'd told her often enough not to woolgather when she was out, not now.

She castigated herself again and started to pay more attention. Traffic was starting to pick up along the streets leading to campus, and a thought struck her.

"Shouldn't we be driving instead of walking?"

"Why?"

"Well, I feel like a target right now."

"You'd be as much of a target in your car if that's where they want to get you. No, we're going to change it up, in case they're watching. Walk some days, drive some days. They'll have to find another way if they can't predict."

"They could just wait."

He glanced down at her, a faint smile easing his face. "Yes, they could."

She stopped walking to face him. At once he grabbed her hand and started them going again.

"Max!"

"Shh. Not so loud. Maybe you should call me Ken now."

"Like I'll remember."

"Just don't hold still. It makes for an easier target. What were you going to give me hell about?"

She had to take a moment to remember. "Oh, yeah. If they can just wait and pick their time, what difference does it make if we switch things out?"

"If we take a different way to the campus every day, we might frustrate them a bit."

"A frustrated assassin is good?"

"Always. The more their emotions come into play, the more likely they are to make a mistake."

Well, she guessed that was true. Look at the mistakes her emotions had caused her to make.

"Somehow," she said, "I don't think we should be out in the open at all."

"If I could find a way to avoid it, I would. Same problem with that as leaving town. Are you ready to stay home all the time and lose your job?"

"No," she admitted. "How do you think they're most likely to come after you?"

"I don't know."

"Sniper?" God, she couldn't believe they were discussing this.

"If they find me, maybe. But I can be pretty hard to find when I want."

"You do look different." The glasses totally changed his appearance, and she noticed he was walking differently.

"And I'm going to look even more different after I leave you at class."

"How so?"

"Amazing what you can do by stuffing a little eraser in your cheeks."

"And why are you walking differently?"

"Because a person's stride can be identified even when he changes everything else."

"The things I never thought of."

The back of her neck was prickling now as she realized at some deep level that the games were over, that reality was approaching and that this was going to be no movie. In fact, the stuff of movies had come right into her life.

"I feel like I'm being watched," she murmured.

"You are. There are a couple of girls over there to the right. Probably admiring your outfit."

Yeah, her brassy outfit that had only been meant to be seen on a dance floor. "You're sure it's not them?"

"I recognize them. Just students. You want me to stay in class with you?"

For an instant she had a wild, overwhelming urge to say yes. She was getting really afraid, at long last. Afraid as she somehow hadn't been before.

"No," she said finally. "I'll be safe in class. You do whatever you need to."

"Okay. I'll be right outside your classroom ten minutes before you're done."

She clung to that, because she was beginning to feel there was nothing else to cling to.

After he left Liza safely in her classroom with nearly a dozen students, Max slipped down the hall to the men's room. Once inside, he pulled out some putty erasers he'd bought, broke them and kneaded them into shape, then stuck them into his mouth between his lower jaw and cheek. His own mother wouldn't recognize him now, he thought as he studied himself in the mirror.

He placed a call to Gage and learned that no one had mentioned seeing any strangers, but he and Micah and Nate were out prowling the entire town, looking for anything at all unusual.

As satisfied as he could be, he set out to walk around the campus, taking care to hunch one shoulder and put a bit of hesitation in his gait. When he had passed by several of his students without being greeted, he felt the job was good enough. They barely glanced at him.

In his mind he had a mental map of the campus, of the places that would be best for a sniper, or an ambush. As of now, he was going to start checking them out regularly.

These guys weren't stupid. They might decide to wait until they felt no one was expecting them. But they could also decide that moving faster would give them the element of surprise.

He wondered which they were going to use against him, and just hoped none of their plans yet involved Liza.

He'd never forgive himself if she got hurt.

Chapter 11

The problem with being on high alert was that time dragged. Max sometimes felt like groaning as the day meandered by. He got Liza to her three o'clock class and then started his wanderings again, wondering how long he was going to be able to keep himself at the needed pitch. Days? Weeks?

Damn, he wished the timeline weren't so lengthy.

But he kept walking, paying attention to everyone he glimpsed. He was sure he'd recognize the guys he was looking for because one thing they hadn't learned to do was change their strides. Makeup, yes. Hair, yes. Clothing, yes. But not the most important thing that could give them away: the way they walked.

It was working well enough for him right now. No one was paying him the least attention, even the coterie of female students who'd been giving him the eye.

He could keep watch while allowing his mind to

wander a bit, however. It was sort of a widened focus, causing him to zoom in visually only when something demanded his attention.

So he thought about Liza, and all the things he still wanted to know about her. All the questions he hadn't had a chance to ask, and all the answers he still wanted to hear. He just hoped they'd get the opportunity.

If she didn't ditch him after all this. Something had sure ticked her off last night, and he didn't have a clue what it was. He hoped she would get around to telling him.

The cell phone in his pocket buzzed, and he made his way to a quiet spot. Only two people could be calling him, Liza and Ames.

It was Ames. "Max, they know about Liza Enders."

He froze. His heart seemed to stop. "You're sure?"

"Would I call otherwise? Mitch, one of our geeks, said someone picked up the trail of her searches. He doesn't know how."

Max remained frozen for another second, then he started walking again, checking every likely place for an ambush. Damn it, there were only a dozen buildings, and the foliage around the place wasn't all that thick. Inside. They'd have to act inside.

"You suspected that last night."

"Now Mitch is sure."

"All right."

"Max, we can get a dozen guys in there."

"Not without scaring them off. Have you seen this place?"

Ames fell silent. "You're the judge," he said finally. "But while the whole town might recognize strangers, the bad guys won't."

"Like it isn't stamped all over most of our agents.

Man, Ames, you know how most of us stand out. Have you got a bunch of guys you can send me who have been undercover long enough to blend here?"

Ames didn't reply, which was answer enough.

"Right," Max said. "Too many of us practically have U.S. Government stamped on our foreheads. I'd need six sunburned, windburned cowboys. Got any of those?"

Again, no answer.

"Okay," Max said. "So there's no question they know about Liza. I just want you to do one thing for me."

"What?"

"Find out who the hell the leak is."

Ames was silent for a second. "I'm looking, Max. Believe me, it's one of the main things on my mind. But you know the problem with that."

Indeed he did. Picking up the leak might tip the militants off. He disconnected, glanced at his watch and saw it was time to go meet Liza. He had to force himself to move slowly and maintain the hitch in his gait.

Five minutes later he looked into the maw of hell. Liza's class sat in their desks and Liza was gone.

The fire alarm went off. Liza looked up from the overhead projector immediately and saw astonishment on the faces of her class.

"Don't move," she told her class.

The school had run her through the procedures when she'd first taken her position. Check outside the classroom to make sure the hall is safe…

"Let me check the hall," she added, when she saw the first flutter of panic. "I need to make sure there's a safe exit. Every one of these doors is a fire door, remember?"

They probably didn't remember. Maybe they'd never been told.

"If I don't come back," she said just before she opened the door, "you're safest here. Just wait. The fire department will come soon."

She stepped out into the hallway, listening to the door closing behind her. Another teacher stepped out farther down the hall.

"I don't smell any smoke," he said.

"Me, either. You check those stairs and I'll check these."

He headed one way and she headed the other. Still no smoke. Probably one of the students had thrown the alarm as a joke. Still, she had to check the first floor.

A young woman came up behind her and said, "I don't see any fire down there." She looked like a student, clad in jeans with a denim jacket tossed over her arm and a backpack hanging from her other shoulder.

The alarm turned off.

"Okay, thanks," Liza said. "Must have been a false alarm." She couldn't place the woman but that didn't mean anything. While she was getting to the point where she recognized almost everyone on campus, she didn't know every single face yet.

She turned to climb the stairs and reassure her class, then follow the next step: usher them out safely just in case.

She never got that far. Almost as soon as she turned her back, she felt something hard press into her side, near her kidney.

"I'm armed," said the woman. "And you're coming with me."

Liza froze for an instant, trying to remember everything Max had taught her about self-defense. If she moved just right, she ought to be able to push the woman down the stairs behind her.

But there was a gun, and right at that moment one of her male students appeared above her. "Is everything okay, Liza?"

"You were supposed to stay in the room, Jeff."

"Yeah, but everybody's freaking."

"Go back and tell them it's okay. False alarm. I just need to go do something downstairs."

"Okay. Are we done with class?"

"Wait five. If I'm not back by then, it means we're done for the day."

"You got it."

He turned to go and Liza realized the woman had moved and now stood well below her on the stairs. Bad position. If she threw herself at the woman, she'd probably get shot and end up with a broken neck, too.

"Turn around and head down. If you behave you won't get hurt."

Liza obeyed because she didn't have any alternative. She could only hope that she'd have a better opportunity later.

If only she could warn Max.

She went meekly enough because of the gun, because the woman holding it didn't get close enough for her to act. The woman backed rapidly down the stairs, stepped to one side to make plenty of room for Liza, her denim jacket still concealing her forearm and weapon. But Liza could see that ugly borehole pointing directly at her.

When Liza reached the bottom of the stairs, she was motioned outside where dangers increased. She would have tried to slam the door between herself and the woman, but these doors had pneumatic closers that made slamming them impossible.

Liza's mouth felt as dry as desert sand, and her palms were wet. She licked her lips, looking for a means of escape, a way to fight, but even if she could think of something, there were too many young people walking around campus. She couldn't risk one of them becoming an innocent victim if the woman behind her started shooting.

Her heart hammered so loudly she hardly heard greetings called to her.

"Go to the new building," said the woman behind her.

The new building. It hadn't yet been opened for classes as it still needed some interior finishing. The work crews hadn't been around lately, and she was willing to bet there wouldn't be another soul there.

Her gaze desperately searching for Max, she walked. Away from where he would look for her. Away from anywhere he was likely to be. She wondered what was going to happen next, and was terrified that Max would walk into a trap—a trap she was determined not to be part of.

They were here. Understanding ran like fire through Max's brain as Liza's students all babbled at once about the fire alarm and how she'd gone out to check.

They were here.

He tried to force himself to be calm, to kick his mind into gear and separate himself from his feelings. It was a well-used trick, one he was good at, but never before had it been this difficult. Divorcing his emotions from Liza's jeopardy seemed well nigh impossible.

He told the class to settle down and stay—it might be

dangerous outside for a little while. He was surprised that they did it.

Then he closed his eyes, summoning his mental map of the campus, and reached a conclusion: they'd try to lure him to the empty building. Nobody would be there. They'd be able to set up a perimeter, and get him when he entered.

And they had Liza. They knew he'd be looking for her.

Calm settled over him. That crew had no idea how dangerous he could be. Flexing his hands, he set out.

Liza started thinking about fighting again as soon as they got into the empty building. If she could just get close enough to the woman…

But her hopes were dashed when a rough-looking man appeared from a room to the right.

"Let's get her upstairs," he said. He, too, had a gun.

Not now, Liza thought. *Not now.* Two guns, and two people, one who ascended the stairwell first then aimed his gun at her and motioned her to come up. The woman followed at a safe distance.

They herded her into a room. She scanned it quickly, noticing drywall scraps, a couple of buckets, a lot of dust and an open window. An open second-floor window. Did she have the nerve?

She turned and faced her captors, deciding to go on the attack. "What the hell is this about?" she demanded. "Who are you guys?"

"You don't need to know who we are," the woman answered. "All you have to do is call Max."

"Call who?"

"Don't play stupid," the man snapped. "You've been hunting him online."

"You mean the guy who just started teaching here?" Liza said, hoping her voice was steady enough and that they couldn't see the tremors of apprehension she could feel in her muscles. Where was the damn adrenaline when she needed it?

"Don't play dumb," the woman said.

"I'm not dumb," Liza retorted and stepped back a little, hoping to lull them into thinking she just wanted to be as far from those guns as possible. Which, come to think of it, was true.

"You know him," the man said. "You were checking him out."

"I'm a reporter. I get curious. I just wanted to know who he was. And why does that get a gun pointed at me? What the hell has he done? I couldn't find out anything. Is he some kind of criminal? Are you cops?"

Another step toward the window. She hoped when the time came she had the nerve to jump, or at least to toss something out to warn Max exactly where they were.

The woman changed tack, her voice gentling. "All we want is to find him. You can help us do that."

"How? I don't know where he is!" Anger was better than fear, and she was revving up a really good mad right now, still wondering when the adrenaline would arrive. Maybe that was what was making her so angry.

"Then," said the woman, "maybe you'd better call him and tell him we're going to kill you if he doesn't get over here fast."

Liza swallowed hard. Her heart seemed to have climbed into her throat. "No," she said.

The man waved his gun. "No?"

"No. If you kill me, I'll never call him for you, will I?"

That's when the man stepped menacingly toward

her. "We can make you call him. And believe me, you won't refuse for long."

Liza wished she didn't believe him. Her knees weakened at the look in his gaze, as if he would enjoy every second of hurting her.

Oh, God. She had to let Max know where they were. No matter what. He'd come looking for her and walk into a trap. But how?

And then the adrenaline hit and hit hard. She ran for the window.

Max walked in a tightening spiral, working his way in toward the new building. Regardless of whether the trap was inside or out, they'd be out here watching for his arrival. Careful to keep to his odd gait, he lowered his head a bit and kept watch through his eyebrows.

He knew every possible hiding spot and was sure at least some of them would be keeping watch outside.

He found the first of them five minutes later. Five minutes of terror for Liza. He tried not to think about that. Couldn't think about that now. He had to stay focused.

The guy was standing beside some newly planted trees, dressed like most of the students in jeans, T-shirt and athletic shoes. He was smoking a cigarette, leaning against one of the saplings, a stack of textbooks at his feet. Just like a student.

Except Max recognized him. He hadn't even changed his haircut, the jerk. Max shuffled up to him, keeping his head down, catching the exact moment when the guy looked at him and dismissed him. Good.

An instant later he sprang, swung the guy around and gave him a throat chop. "Why, hello, Shades," he said.

Shades's eyes widened even as he clutched his throat and fell, trying to breathe.

"Too bad I didn't kill you."

Shades gurgled.

"Lucky you, you'll breathe again. Eventually." Squatting, he searched Shades and found a pistol and a radio. He smashed the radio and kept the pistol. Then he went through Shades's other pockets and found some useful stuff. Plastic ties and a bandanna.

Either they'd planned to take Liza away, or they'd planned to have some fun with him before killing him. Not so bright. They should have taken him out with a sniper.

Of course, maybe they'd had a little trouble figuring out who he was the past couple of days.

Whatever, right now he didn't much care. He had to get to Liza, and he had to do it in one piece so he could help her.

He tied Shades up, gagged him with the bandanna, and once he was sure the guy couldn't move, kicked leaves over him to conceal him.

He took just enough time to call Gage. "They're here on campus. They've got Liza. I just took one out about two hundred yards from the new building. He's under a pile of leaves, north side."

Then he switched off his phone and resumed hunting.

Liza got her legs outside the window before they grabbed her. Two of them seized her arms in bruising grips, the woman's nails digging into her. She fought, trying to get her butt over the ledge, but they began to drag her back inside.

She screamed in anger and rage, struggling, but she

hadn't lost her senses. By the time they dragged her back inside, she'd managed to kick off the Mary Janes Max had noticed just this morning. He'd get the message.

But that didn't mean she was going to stop fighting. While they were holding her, they couldn't shoot her. She struck out like a wildcat with everything she had: feet, hands, fingers, going for knees and eyes as Max had taught her.

Then she received an ear-ringing blow to the side of her head, and for just an instant everything went black.

The next thing she knew, she'd been hurled into a corner like a rag doll. When she could see again, she was staring at two very angry people with guns.

Not good.

"Tie her up," the guy said.

The woman shrugged. "I can shoot her just as easily. But maybe not yet. She's our ace."

"You don't know that. Maybe she *was* just a curious reporter."

The woman glared at him. "Max is ATF. You think he's gonna leave an innocent to our mercies? He'll come. Just as soon as he realizes that she's in trouble."

Liza shook her head a bit to clear it, and started slowly drawing her bare feet under her. Well, she thought, they knew Max all right. He'd come.

The woman turned back to her. "Slide your cell phone to me now, unless you want another wallop in the head."

Liza pretended a klutziness and confusion she wasn't feeling, hoping they'd mistake her as concussed. Or more concussed than she was. She fumbled at pockets until the annoyed sighs the woman made began to sound too impatient.

She shoved the phone toward them, knowing they wouldn't find anything. Because Max had made her put him under a different name.

The woman took the phone and scanned the directory. Liza gathered herself even more.

"No Max," the woman said disgustedly. "No Max, no Ken, no nothing."

"Double negative," Liza said, deliberately slurring her words.

The man swore. "Shut the hell up."

So she shut up, for now.

"What now?" the man demanded. "We've got your hostage and no way to know if Max gives a damn."

"I told you, he gives a damn. Crap, Joe, they were on his motorcycle together just a few days ago."

At that, Liza's heart froze. How long had they been watching? Did they know Max had changed his appearance?

Her mind began to scramble wildly for solutions. Any solutions.

Max took out the second guy as easily as the first. They were looking for someone they recognized, and they didn't recognize him now at all.

But that left at least two more, maybe four, and he was sure now they were inside the building. Reinforcements hadn't arrived yet, but it hadn't been that long.

When he heard Liza's scream, his heart seized. Anger threatened to swamp him and he had to force it down to keep his mind clear. He rounded the other side of the building.

Then he spied the shoes beneath the window. Liza's electric-blue shoes. Looking up, he saw the open window. Shuffling, trying to look disabled, he headed toward the door of the building.

The instant he stepped inside, he found another two. And just as he'd hoped, they didn't recognize him.

"Get out," one of them said menacingly. Max recognized him as the guy who went by the nickname Klondike.

"Huh?" He stood, pretending stupidity and surprise, until they moved toward him to make him leave.

Then he took advantage of all the explosive speed he'd learned getting that black belt he hadn't told Liza he had.

They weren't expecting it, which made it so damn easy. He moved in a blur, disarming them and then taking them down. They fell like startled marionettes who'd lost their strings. He was pretty sure he'd dislocated one guy's knee. Maybe he'd done both of them. The sound hadn't been pretty.

They lay there unconscious now, but he wasn't going to rely on that. He used the ties from their own pockets, trussing them good. And now he didn't care if they woke up and screamed bloody murder.

Two more, most likely. Two more. And he knew exactly where they were.

With Liza.

Liza heard the commotion downstairs. Some thuds. Maybe a groan. She pushed to her feet, leaning heavily on the wall, pretending she needed the support, while the other two looked toward the door.

"He's coming," the man said.

"Yeah. Or they got him."

Neither of them, Liza realized, was quite ready to

believe that. So she sought a distraction. "I'm going to be sick," she moaned.

"Shut up," the man said. He barely glanced away from the door.

"I need a bucket," she insisted, making her voice thick as if she were indeed about to vomit.

"Do it on the floor," the woman snapped.

Liza bent over, holding her stomach, scanning for anything harder than a piece of drywall. She found it at last, a piece of two-by-two, about eighteen inches long. She edged toward it, making retching sounds.

Now they were ignoring her completely, figuring she was too sick to be a threat. She grabbed the piece of wood and tucked it under her arm lengthwise. She made herself retch again.

Then the door opened and a man stood there. Liza almost didn't recognize him, his face looked so different.

"Nobody's supposed to be up here," Max said almost dully. Then he seemed to notice their guns.

"Hey, what are those for?" He stepped into the room and they both aimed at him.

"Get the hell out," the woman said. "Or I'll shoot you, so help me."

Max shook his head and shuffled even closer. The woman lifted her gun and aimed.

Liza flew into action. In just a single step, she reached the woman's side and brought the wood down on her forearm with every bit of strength she had. The gun clattered to the floor.

At that moment Max turned into a ninja. He swung his leg in a fast, high arc, disarming the other guy, and then moved in. Liza wasn't about to miss her chance. She hit the woman again and kicked the gun away.

Damn it, it didn't go far enough. She hit the woman on the side of the head as hard as she could. The woman's legs buckled. Liza went for the pistol and picked it up, pointing it at the woman.

Suddenly everything was quiet except for heavy breathing. Max stood poised as if he wasn't ready to give up the fight.

Then a lazy voice drawled from the doorway, "We seem to be a little late."

Liza turned her head and saw Nate, Micah and Gage. Adrenaline chose that moment to desert her. Her knees gave way, and she sank to the floor, still holding the gun.

Chapter 12

Liza stood barefoot on the grass and watched the six bad guys get loaded, handcuffed, into ambulances. Max had done quite a number on them. Well, except for the woman. Liza had done that number herself, and at the moment she wasn't regretting it.

Max was pacing, his face and his stride back to normal, as he talked on the phone.

Liza had already given her statement to Gage, and there were enough deputies, students and firemen around to make the area feel like a county fair. At least there were no TV cameras, although she supposed there were enough cell phone cameras documenting the events. Her hands were absolutely itching for a notebook and pencil. She wanted to write the article about this, to be right in the thick of it.

Except she was a participant, and as a reporter she knew that was forbidden.

Would she ever leave those instincts behind?

She rubbed her upper arms a little, feeling the growing bruises. At least the woman's nails hadn't drawn blood, thanks to her shirt, but she suspected she would discover even more bruises before the day was over.

Well, if that was the worst that happened, she was lucky.

At long last, Max came to join her.

"What's up?" she asked, her thirst for information as intense as ever.

"ATF will be out here to get these guys tomorrow. That pretty much will sew up the case. And Ames pulled down the leak. You were right."

"I was?" The idea both pleased and startled her.

"That woman you just took out, Rose, she got some liquor into one of our geeks after he announced he was working on a big case. She flattered him just right and he gave her my real name, and told her about you hunting for me. Once they were on it, they didn't have trouble locating you."

"How did she find him to begin with?"

"In Washington it's hard not to bump into someone in the government, and there are a few places that are the equivalent of cop bars, if you know what I mean."

"So she homed in on the likeliest places to find someone from ATF."

"Yeah. And it was easy because she's a computer geek herself, so she directed the conversation that way. Pretty good. It only took her a month to latch onto Mitch."

Liza knew how easy it was to get people to talk when you found the right angle for flattery. "Wow."

"A month to latch onto him, and only a couple of weeks to convince him she was in love with him and adored him and he fell for it. He wanted to impress her. Fortunately for us, he started to feel guilty about it a few weeks ago and started hinting to Ames that something was wrong."

"I guess he'll never be a field agent now."

"He's going to be lucky, I think. Ames is considering just firing him rather than charging him."

"How do you feel about that?"

He shrugged. "It's important to plug the leak. God knows how many other cases this guy was part of."

Liza nodded, but thinking it over she realized she might have been manipulated in the same way that Rose had manipulated Mitch. Max had said it was his duty to protect her. Maybe protecting her had been a whole lot easier because of her attraction to him.

She couldn't exactly blame him, but she felt soiled by the thought. And angry.

"If you don't need me, I'm going home."

He nodded, his polar-blue eyes searching her face. "Okay. I'll see you in a little while."

Yeah, she thought as she grabbed her shoes from the ground nearby and shoved her feet into them. He'd come by to let her down as gently as he could, tell her it had been great but he had to go to Washington or wherever and get back to being an ATF agent.

Oh, yeah. She could feel it coming.

Battling a sudden urge to cry, she walked home as fast as she could. When she got into her apartment, all she could see were signs of Max everywhere. She wanted to pack his things up, but a stubborn streak reared and she decided to let him do it all himself.

Instead she stepped out onto her balcony, into the chilling air of the autumn evening, and sat, waiting for doom to arrive at her door.

No amount of arguing with herself could make her feel any better. There'd been no talk of a future, no indication whatsoever that Max wouldn't leave as soon as this was wrapped up.

She couldn't see him hanging around to teach. Not that man. He might never want to go undercover again, but she knew all too well how hard it was to give up the adrenaline rush of being on a big story or a big case.

She loved this town and liked her new job, but it didn't give her the excitement she so thrived on. At least not until Max had come into her life.

She had enough adjusting to do herself, and none of it was by choice. She could hardly imagine him wanting to do the same thing, not when he still had options.

She cried a bit, but not too much. The ache in her chest constricted the tears. Was it possible to hurt too badly to weep? Evidently so.

She'd leaped before she had looked, and she couldn't blame anyone but herself for that.

Night had fallen completely by the time she heard the key turn in the lock.

"Liza?"

"Out here on the balcony." At least she sounded normal, not like someone facing the end of a hope, a dream.

He didn't turn on any lights, simply made his way through the dark apartment. Half a minute later he sat on the plastic chair beside her.

"Are you okay?" he asked.

"Sure." A lie. "Why?"

"Because you're sitting out here in the dark and cold."

"It's a nice night." Yeah, the night was nice. What

was about to happen, not so much. When he didn't speak she asked, "So when are you leaving?"

"I have to go back to Washington tomorrow with the prisoners."

Her heart sank all the way to her toes. "Witness?"

"Again." He paused. "You have to come with me."

"I already gave my statement."

"You know how agencies are. Everyone wants to take their own affidavit."

"I guess."

He fell quiet again, then finally said, "Liza? Is it so awful to go to Washington with me?"

"No. Why would it be?"

Another pause, then, "Liza, for God's sake, what's wrong? What did I do? Since last night you've barely been able to look at me."

For someone who almost had something to say, she was finding it incredibly difficult to talk, as if lead weighted her tongue and lips. If the only thing she had left to preserve was her pride, then preserve it she would.

"Liza?"

She just shook her head.

But that didn't stop him. He reached for her and pulled her close, kissing her hard and deep. Her heart leaped, then she ripped herself away, unable to bear anymore.

"You finished your job," she said thickly, looking away.

"My job?" He sounded honestly shocked. Then he apparently understood. "You think *that* was about my job?"

Anger flared, coming to her rescue. "Of course it

was. It was all about your duty to protect me. You said so yourself."

He swore savagely and she almost winced. It wasn't that she hadn't heard the words before—she'd heard worse, in fact—but the violence with which he enunciated them caught her off guard.

"Do you think I'm a jerk?" he asked, his voice tight with anger.

"I didn't say that!"

"You all but implied it. So you really think I slept with you as part of protecting you? You think that was all some kind of lie so I could control you? What the hell do you take me for?"

He grabbed her hand and tugged her inside her apartment, slamming the sliding glass door so hard the wall shook. "Tell me, Liza. Tell me to my face that I'm nothing but a conscienceless user."

She gulped and looked up at him. His eyes had become blue flames of fury. The anger on his face should have terrified her, but oddly it comforted her.

"I don't really know you," she said.

"No, and if you keep this up, you never will. But there's one thing I can promise you here and now. I have never used a woman the way you're suggesting I used you. Not once. Not ever."

She wanted to believe it. She really did. "But you said…"

"I was talking about the other situation, not us. Most definitely not us."

He caught her chin in his hand, making her look at him. "Tell me you believe me, because if you don't I'm out of here now."

"But if I do?"

"Then we're going to have a wonderful time in D.C.

and we're going to take time to get to know each other, and Liza, I'm hoping against hope that you might actually come to love me."

"Love you?" She almost stuttered the words because she had convinced herself that love between them was impossible.

"Love me," he said firmly. "The way I already love you."

Shock ripped through her. Of all the things she had expected, that wasn't it. She went by turns hot and cold, and then started to sway. Not possible.

Max's powerful arms wrapped around her, steadying her. "Liza? Are you okay? I know it's been a hard, scary day but I didn't… Look, you don't have to get upset because of *my* feelings. I can get that you don't share them. It…"

She hushed him by lifting her face to kiss him. She felt him stiffen, then his hold on her tightened. "I love you," she whispered. "Oh, my God, how I love you!"

"Really? Honestly?"

Then he threw back his head and let out a *yeehaw* that could probably be heard in every apartment in the building. She started to laugh.

He grinned down at her. "It's going to be so great, Liza. I promise. No more undercover work for me, I swear. You want to keep teaching, I'll be here every weekend until I get things sorted out at work. Then we can…"

He hesitated, looking deep into her eyes. "We'll figure it all out. We'll work it out. Because I want to be with you every day for the rest of my life. I want us to have a family—are kids okay?"

"Shh," she said, touching his mouth with her hand and feeling tears of joy sting in her eyes. "Shh. There's plenty of time, now. Plenty of time. We can work it all out later."

He seemed to agree, because he swept her up into his arms and carried her back to the bedroom. As soon as they tangled together on the bed she was absolutely certain of one thing:

They had both figured out where they belonged. And it was here. Forever.

* * * * *

SUSPENSE

COMING NEXT MONTH
AVAILABLE APRIL 24, 2012

#1703 HER HERO AFTER DARK
H.O.T. Watch
Cindy Dees

#1704 THE PERFECT OUTSIDER
Perfect, Wyoming
Loreth Anne White

#1705 TEXAS MANHUNT
Chance, Texas
Linda Conrad

#1706 IT STARTED THAT NIGHT
Virna DePaul

REQUEST YOUR FREE BOOKS!
2 FREE NOVELS PLUS 2 FREE GIFTS!

Harlequin®

ROMANTIC
SUSPENSE

Sparked by Danger, Fueled by Passion.

*Colby Investigator Lyle McCaleb is on the case.
But can he protect Sadie Gilmore from her haunting past?*

*Harlequin Intrigue® presents a new installment
in Debra Webb's miniseries,* COLBY, TX.

Enjoy a sneak peek of COLBY LAW.

With the shotgun hanging at her side, she made it as far as the porch steps, when the driver's side door opened. Sadie knew the deputies in Coryell County. Her visitor wasn't any of them. A boot hit the ground, stirring the dust. Something deep inside her braced for a new kind of trouble. As the driver emerged, Sadie's gaze moved upward, over the gleaming black door and the tinted window to a black Stetson and dark sunglasses. She couldn't quite make out the details of the man's face but some extra sense that had nothing to do with what she could see set her on edge.

Another boot hit the ground and the door closed. Her visual inspection swept over long legs cinched in comfortably worn denim, a lean waist and broad shoulders testing the seams of a shirt that hadn't come off the rack at any store where she shopped, finally zeroing in on the man's face just as he removed the dark glasses.

The weapon almost slipped from her grasp. Her heart bucked hard twice, then skidded to a near halt.

Lyle McCaleb.

"What the...devil?" whispered past her lips.

Unable to move a muscle, she watched in morbid fascination as he hooked the sunglasses on to his hip pocket and strode toward the house—toward her. Sadie wouldn't have been able to summon a warning that he was trespassing had her life depended on it.

Lyle glanced at the shotgun as he reached up and removed his hat. "Expecting company?"

As if her heart had suddenly started to pump once more, kicking her brain into gear, fury blasted through her frozen muscles. "What do you want, Lyle McCaleb?"

"Seeing as you didn't know I was coming, that couldn't be for me." He gave a nod toward her shotgun.

This could not be happening. Seven years he'd been gone. This was…this was… "I have nothing to say to you." She turned her back to him and walked away. Who did he think he was, showing up here like this after all this time? It was crazy. He was crazy!

"I know I'm the last person on this earth you want to see."

Her feet stopped when she wanted to keep going. To get inside the house and slam the door and dead bolt it.

"We need to talk."

The stakes are high as Lyle fights for the woman he loves. But can he solve the case in time to save an innocent life?

Find out in COLBY LAW
Available May 2012 from Harlequin Intrigue®
wherever books are sold.